This novel is entirely a work of fiction

The names, characters and incidents portrayed in it are the work of the author's imagination and any resemblance to actual persons, living or dead, events or localities is entirely coincidental.

First Edition (1.2) 04/01/2018

Dedication

To my granddaughter Eden, who is the apple of my eye who deserves to have the most amazing destiny of her own, outside of fiction. Written with love...

Eden and the Key of Destiny

Chapter 1

Battersea, London. Thirteen years ago.

It was a filthy December night. The rain lashed down heavily, driven by the cold easterly wind that cut to the bone. A small portly man, wearing a smart raincoat, entered the cobbled street that led down to the River Thames. He carried a large wicker basket in one hand and an official looking briefcase in the other. The rather strange little man was having the greatest difficulty in managing them both in the strong gusty wind. He wore a bowler hat, which threatened to take off in the stiff breeze, above rain splattered wire spectacles. He had a cane walking stick jammed under his arm and wore the most amazing handlebar moustache. The little man was clearly a gentleman of some importance.

The rather unusual little man hurried down the cobbled lane, turning to look behind him from time to time. It was as if he was frightened of being followed. He stopped outside an old red-bricked building and looked around once again for any onlookers. There were none and the dapper little man gave a heavy sigh at the relief of it. The sign above the grand old doorway was weathered and faded.

"*Battersea Home for Children*," it said, almost apologetically.

Satisfied that nobody was watching him, the rather strange little man ducked into the porch. Seconds later, he reappeared and hurried on in the direction he had been going, still checking behind for unwanted observers. The basket was gone though, leaving his hand free to carry his cane once more. The gentleman disappeared into the night until all that could be heard, was the distant tapping of his cane on the stone cobbles. His fleeting visit to the orphanage was as if it had never happened.

The milkman stopped his van in front of the red-bricked building at five o'clock in the morning. The rain had turned to heavy snow in the night and his wheels were the first to leave their tracks on the road. The orphanage always had the same milk order; five litres, from Monday to Friday, and ten on Saturday. Today was Saturday. The old grey haired milkman took ten cartons from his van and trudged through the shin deep snow to the front door of the orphanage.

The strong winds had drifted the soft snow into the porch, so that it was over knee deep. The milkman dropped his heavy package into the corner, where it sank almost completely out of sight in the soft snow. He was about to leave, when he heard the sound of a baby crying close by. The milkman looked around the porch, puzzled. He could hear the crying but couldn't see any sign of a baby. Then the crying turned into angry screams, coming from what appeared to be under the snow.

"Nonsense," he thought. "I must be imagining it."

He was about to dismiss it as just his imagination, when the screaming got louder still. The old man began to scrape the snow away. He worked slowly at first and then urgently as he realised that there was a baby there; somewhere. Seconds later, he had uncovered a basket. The milkman pulled the lace veil from it cautiously and was confronted with the strangest sight. It was a baby looking blue with cold, but somehow red with rage too. As young as it was, the little mite was clearly angry at having been so rudely dumped there.

The milkman picked up the basket, brushed it off and gave the doorbell a long ring. It took several minutes before he could hear footsteps inside and the baby screamed petulantly throughout. The big oak door finally creaked open on old rusty hinges and the baby hushed at the sudden noise of it. A young, fresh-faced woman appeared at the doorway. She wore a blue nurse's uniform and white nursing cap. She had owl-like glasses, ginger hair and just the sweetest smile.

"Good morning Joe," she greeted.

"Good morning to you Phoebe," he returned her smile. "Christmas has come early it would seem."

"The snow, you mean?" Phoebe guessed.

"No, I mean this."

The milkman offered the wicker basket. Phoebe's astonishment was immense as she stared disbelievingly at the baby through those owl-like eyes. The baby just giggled back at her, having never seen anything of the like.

"How, I mean where?" Phoebe was lost for words.

"She was buried in the snow just there in the corner. I heard her crying," Joe pointed, handing over the basket.

"She?" Phoebe asked. "You know the baby then?" the young nurse was disorientated and missing the obvious.

"No, just dressed in pink and smells of roses. That's usually a little girl, isn't it?" he grinned broadly, then chuckled.

"Yes, of course," Phoebe replied, feeling a little embarrassed over her silly question. "Thank you."

"She must have been there all night," Joe pointed out, "there's no footsteps in the snow you see."

"Quite," Phoebe agreed, "in which case she must be hungry then. I'll feed her and then call the police to see if they can find her mother."

Phoebe said goodbye to Joe and took the baby to the kitchen. It was early, so the children living there were still in their beds. Breakfast wasn't due for another two hours. That meant she would have time enough to bath and feed the baby. Phoebe set the basket on the kitchen table and un-wrapped the baby. Just at that moment, Lucy walked in. She was also a young nurse, in her late teens; slim and pretty, with long black hair piled high and a cheeky smile.

“Who has brought us roses?” she asked, overwhelmed by the sweet perfume.

Phoebe stood aside, revealing the baby swaddled in a pink blanket. Lucy’s jaw dropped in amazement.

“Where did *she* come from?”

“The milkman found her in the porch, buried under the snow. She's so lovely and for some reason, she smells of roses,” Lucy looked proud to have the little bundle.

“Lovely? Oh my goodness isn't she just!”

Lucy picked her up and was immediately rewarded with a smile and a giggle.

“She’s so cold,” Lucy noticed. “We need to bath her straight away to warm her up.”

They were both too busy cooing over the baby to notice Mrs Jones walk in; a bland, middle aged woman, with shoulder length salt and pepper hair and glasses. More than this, she was the boss and not a very kind one at that. All the children at the orphanage hated her; the staff too.

"What's this?" Mrs Jones bellowed, pointing an accusing finger at the little pink bundle.

"A baby girl with nowhere to go," Phoebe replied, defensively.

Phoebe held the baby protectively against her. Mrs Jones was a hard and cruel woman. Phoebe knew just how quickly this woman could turn nasty and continued hurriedly.

"The m-milkman found her in the porch, buried in the snow. She hasn't got anybody, you see. Anyway, we could look after her until...."

Mrs Jones raised a hand to silence Phoebe.

"Listen! I don't want to see her or hear her. Keep her away from me," Mrs Jones spat the words out hatefully, sniffing the air that was filled with the fragrance of roses, and then added disdainfully. "Nor smell her!"

Mrs Jones stormed out of the room muttering and shaking her head in annoyance.

"It has begun. I knew there would be more trouble," she said and strutted off to the solitude of her own personal tower.

With Mrs Jones gone, Phoebe and Lucy bathed the baby, chatting animatedly as they did so.

“She didn't mention getting rid of her, only that she didn't want to see her, hear her or smell her,” Phoebe confirmed, looking perplexed. “What do you make of that Lucy? Mrs Jones absolutely hates babies.”

The baby giggled as she splashed her hands in the bath water, soaking Lucy.

“It can only mean that we are keeping her Phoebe, but I can't think why,” Lucy wondered. “She can sleep in our room though, and we can take turns looking after her. That way, Mrs Jones will never see her; ever.”

The two young women looked thrilled at the idea. They were already in love with the joyous little bundle.

“We can't keep calling her *she*,” Phoebe declared, noticing the little gold necklace around the baby’s neck. “It seems her name is *Eden*,” she added, reading the name plate.

“And there’s a golden key on the chain too. I wonder what lock it opens.” Lucy added.

“I wonder?” Phoebe thought on it for a moment. “It must have been very important. I'm sure if Eden ever finds that lock, it will answer all of her questions.”

"Yes, I think so too," Lucy agreed, "but we must hide the necklace until Eden is older. Mrs Jones will take it away from her, you can be sure of that."

They finished bathing Eden. Oddly though, she still smelled just as strongly of roses, if not more.

"Most strange," Phoebe declared, "but it all helps us name her; how about *Eden Rose Lock*?"

"Perfect!" Lucy agreed. "Now let's get little Miss Lock some breakfast!"

Chapter 2

Battersea, London. Thirteen years later.

And so it was for the next thirteen years. Eden became like a daughter to Phoebe and Lucy and they kept her safely out of the cruel Mrs Jones's sight. It was at a cost though, as Eden could rarely mix with the other children and became lonesome and sad.

She grew to love Phoebe and Lucy as if they were her parents, but always wondered where she was from and who her *real* parents were. More than this, she wondered what she had done that was so dreadful as to make her parents want to give her away. Eden had so many questions and nobody to ask. The pressure of not knowing was building up like volcano inside her and she could barely keep a lid on it.

Right from the start, Eden knew that she was different from the other children though. It was because she could hear their thoughts and they were nothing like hers. She would often say *yes*, before someone called her name. She had glimpses into the future you see, but that wasn't always a good thing. Sometimes, she could even move things without touching them. That was really strange. Eden would have just loved to be the same as the other children, but of course that was simply impossible. She just wasn't.

"I just want to be ordinary, like the other children," Eden said to Phoebe despairingly, as she was getting herself ready for her thirteenth birthday party.

"Why would you want to be *ordinary* Eden, when you are so extraordinary?" Phoebe answered, reinforcing it with an honest smile.

"Because nobody likes *extraordinary*," Eden countered. "I frighten them because I know what they're thinking." then she added with embarrassment. "They say that I smell too."

"But you do Eden," Phoebe agreed. "You smell *beautiful*. They are jealous is all; they would love to smell of roses, rather than antiseptic soap. They are just bullies Eden, ignore them. Bullies go away when you do that."

It was true and Eden knew it, but all every teenager really wants to do is fit in. Eden was a square peg in a round hole. The other children saw her confinement in the nurses' quarters as favouritism. They didn't understand that the captivity and loneliness was unbearable for her.

Eden's party really was going to be a rare treat. It was to be a celebration of becoming a teenager and getting a little more independence. Phoebe and Lucy had arranged to smuggle Eden out of the orphanage to the local McDonald's, for only the third time in her life. Eden had a passion for their chicken nuggets and chips; something that she was never allowed at the orphanage. It was *forbidden fruit* you see and that always tasted the best to Eden!

"Things were going to change, now that she was a teenager," Eden decided, but hadn't a clue how to do it.

There was no question of taking any of the other children from the orphanage to the party, as Mrs Jones would be sure to find out if they did. Instead, Lucy had invited her fourteen year old nephew, Fin, to keep her company. He had spent several years at the orphanage before Lucy's sister, Elouise, had adopted him. Now he went to a local school and had a normal life, something that Eden would have died for.

But first it was time for presents!

One of Phoebe's presents was a simple white dress that fell to Eden's knees. It made her look very grown up and suited her. The tan, open toed sandals that she bought to match had heels too! That was something that Mrs Jones had forbidden. Eden just adored them. Lucy had bought her a matching tan handbag, filled with cosmetics, which completed her new look.

Eden stood in front of the tall mirror and looked at herself. Phoebe and Lucy were stood behind, proud of their creation. Eden's long blonde hair was neatly brushed and shone with youth. She wore a big white Jo-Jo bow, which was currently quite the fashion. Lucy had made Eden's face up, so that her big green eyes looked somehow even bigger. Just a little blusher and pink lipstick completed the young woman look. Eden turned to face the two nurses and threw her arms around them.

"Thank you so much. I'm so happy, I can't tell you!" Eden really was and it shone from her. "I love you so much, don't ever leave me," she pleaded, unnecessarily.

Somehow, her joy always released that strong fragrance of roses and the room was now filled with it.

"There's one more thing that you should have, now that you are a young lady," Lucy said, smiling conspiratorially at Phoebe.

She searched the back of the top shelf of their wardrobe, until she found it.

"Ah, here it is," Lucy said, handing Eden the golden necklace. "You were wearing it when you came here. We hid it so that Mrs Jones couldn't find it, or you would never have seen it."

"It's beautiful and it's got my name on it too. So *Eden* really is my name then?"

Lucy and Phoebe nodded and smiled.

"What is the golden key for?" Eden asked, with a puzzled expression.

"We don't know, but it looks really important and so pretty," Lucy said admiringly. "Perhaps it will unlock the secret of your life one day," she added.

Eden hoped so. She imagined it opening the door to her real home where her parents would be waiting for her with open arms.

"*The Key of Destiny,*" she wished, but knew that was just nonsense. Anyway, it was too small to open a door.

Lucy fastened it around Eden's neck and turned to Phoebe with the strangest expression on her face.

"I don't remember the necklace being anywhere near this big, do you Phoebe?"

"No," Phoebe replied. "Quite the opposite, I seem to remember it being really quite tiny. In fact, I thought Eden might wear it as a bracelet one day. It just shows what you forget over the years, doesn't it?"

It was a question that needed no answer.

“I can't wait to meet Fin!” Eden enthused, changing the subject.

Also, she just couldn't wait to get out of the orphanage. *Her prison*, as she called it. Ten minutes later, Phoebe and Lucy smuggled Eden out through the back door, giggling at the delicious danger of it. They knew that, if Mrs Jones caught them, there would be hell to pay. That thought just seemed to make it all even more exciting!

The taxi was waiting for them and so it was only fifteen minutes later when they walked into McDonald's. Eden looked around disappointedly. There was nobody in there, other than a strange looking little gentleman sat in the corner. He was leaning on a wooden cane that he had set between his feet. The little gentleman wore a bowler hat and waistcoat with a pocket watch, wire spectacles and an amazing handlebar moustache. Beside him was the most important looking leather briefcase Eden had ever seen, with two big brassy locks on it. Somehow he managed to sip coffee past that impressive moustache. After each sip, the dapper little man fastidiously dabbed his mouth and moustache with a paper napkin.

“He didn't look the kind of man to be in McDonald's,” Eden thought idly, then put the matter out of her mind.

“It's still early,” Phoebe said reassuringly. “Everybody’s only just finished work. It’ll get busy soon and Fin will be here, you will see.”

No sooner said, than a tall slim boy with fair hair and an angelic face entered. He looked awkward, as fourteen year olds do. The boy glanced around and immediately spotted his aunt. Not a hard thing to do in an empty restaurant. He crossed over to her, avoiding eye contact with Eden.

“Hello Auntie Lucy,” he said with a boyish smile.

He was clearly embarrassed and immediately looked down at his shoes for the distraction. He studied them as if it was the first time he had ever seen them.

Lucy gave him a public hug and Fin seemed to get visibly smaller the longer it lasted. She made the introductions and sat Fin next to Eden. Fin perched on the furthest edge of his chair away from her, still looking awkward. It didn't worry Eden though, because she could tell exactly what he was thinking, just like she always could.

“They were nice thoughts,” Eden decided, “and he smelt like a sweet shop,” which was nice too.

Fin’s awkwardness slowly melted as he got to know Eden. It was difficult for him being the only boy at the birthday party, of a girl he had never met before. Fin had been dreading it for weeks, but it really wasn't so bad, he decided.

"You smell nice, like roses," Fin said and immediately felt foolish for saying it.

Eden rescued him.

"You do too Fin, but like a sweetshop. I've only ever been to one in my life, but you smell just like that."

"That was a strange thing to smell of," she thought, but didn't say.

"I always have," Fin said, simply. "It doesn't wash off either."

"Me too Fin. It's just us, I guess," Eden shrugged and that was the end of it.

Eden had so many questions to ask; like, "What is it like to have foster parents and live in a real home?" and, "What is it like to go to school with lots of other children?"

The initial awkwardness faded away and they chatted animatedly, while Phoebe and Lucy talked of work and other things that didn't concern them. It came right out of the blue when Fin touched Eden's necklace.

"I've got one of those too," he announced, reaching into the neck of his t-shirt. "Mine says *Fin* though."

Eden was gob-smacked at the surprise of it.

"And you have a golden key too. What is it for?" Eden asked.

"I don't know," he shrugged. "The same thing as yours I guess."

"The keys are slightly different though," Eden noticed. "They must open different locks."

"So they are," Fin confirmed. "I wonder if we will ever know."

"We can only hope Fin. When we find the locks, we might find out who we are and where we belong," Eden had a happy-sad look on her face.

She noticed that the little man with the big moustache was watching and smiling back at them. He now had the rather important looking briefcase on his lap and his chubby fingers were pointing at the two locks on it.

"Fin, that strange little man is watching us. I think he's trying to tell us something. Look, he's pointing at the locks on his briefcase."

Eden touched the key on her necklace and the man nodded and smiled through his thick moustache. He placed a chubby hand on one of the locks. Then she touched Fin's key and he did the same but with the other lock.

Eden and Fin just looked at each other in disbelief. Well it was a mixture of disbelief and fear of the unknown.

“This isn't possible Fin. It can't be. He's just a strange little man. Our keys can't possibly fit his briefcase; can they?”

“There's only one way to find out Eden.”

Fin had a confidence about him that was so different from the awkward boy that Eden had first met. He stood up and encouraged Eden to do the same.

“We’re just going outside for a breath of fresh air. Is that OK Auntie?” Fin asked.

“Yes, but don't go too far. The taxi will be here in twenty minutes,” Lucy said with a smile, pleased that they had both got on so well together.

As they passed the little man on the way out, Fin gave him a discrete nod. Two minutes later, the little man dabbed his mouth with the napkin, picked up his cane and briefcase and walked out of the restaurant.

Eden and Fin were sat at one of the outside tables, when the little man appeared at the door. Before he crossed to them, he looked up and down the street. It was if he was somewhere that he shouldn't be and was afraid of being seen. Satisfied that it was safe, he crossed quickly to them and greeted them with just the biggest smile. He held out his hand to shake.

“I have waited fourteen years for this day and my, haven't you both grown up well?” he said proudly. “Muffins is my name and I am your servant.”

“Mr Muffins? Eden asked, taking his hand and shaking it. She noticed that he smelt of burnt wood.

“No, just Muffins. We only have one name and one smell where we come from. It's how we know and recognise each other,” the rather proper gentleman told them.

“You said *we*, Muffins. Does that mean that Fin and me come from where you do?” Eden asked.

“Oh yes indeed; most definitely, quite so.”

“So who are we and where are we from?” Fin asked suspiciously. It seemed a bit too fantastic to be true.

“We are one of the five Sensors from another world,” Muffins began. “*Fragrances* they call us or smells if you like. Some of us are good and some bad. We live in all places and all times. As long as we are around, people will enjoy their sense of smell. We are the guardian spirits of the source, you see. I and mine, bring the smell of burnt wood to people’s senses, whereas you and your family bring us the smell of sweets Fin. Eden and hers bless us with the smell of roses. If you and your families disappear, then so will those smells.”

“Who are the other four Sensors then?” Eden asked.

“The *Audibles* bring music to our ears,” Muffins began. “The *Rainbows* bring beautiful colours to our eyes. Our taste is by grace of the *Flavours* and touch and emotions are from the *Sensations*. Without us, people wouldn't hear, see, feel, taste or smell anything. The world would be a desolate place. No love and joy, only isolation and fear.”

The little man's face turned serious and conspiratorial. He whispered to them behind his hand.

“There are some who would have us gone, so we must be careful.”

“Is this a joke?” Fin asked.

The strange little gentleman looked offended.

“It's no joke at all Mr Fin,” Muffins said stiffly, twirling the ends of his moustache in his chubby fingers. “Imagine a world without joy. No fragrances to smell or colours to see. Imagine that nothing has taste or there are songs that you can't hear. Imagine that you don't feel the joy of a touch or a kiss. Imagine that you cannot love. No it is no joke and not funny at all Mr Fin.”

Eden sensed the little man's displeasure and reassured him.

“Fin didn't mean any harm Muffins. It's just a little bit hard to believe for us,” Eden placed her hand comfortingly on Muffins’ arm. “Who would have us *gone* and why?”

“The *Murks* would have you gone. They are everywhere; even Mrs Jones is a Murk. They consume joy and feed on misery. It makes them stronger you see. Eventually, when all joy is gone, they will be all powerful and the world will be theirs. A miserable place it will be too.”

“Do you mean they will try to kill us?” Fin asked, still unsure that this wasn't just a practical joke.

“No, they can't do that. It would be a mortal sin, punishable by *the Creator*. The Murks’ way is to imprison you in *the Vacuum*, a sealed place where light, sound and smell can't enter or leave. They can't do that to children though, well at least not until they are sixteen. That would be another mortal sin you see, punishable by the Creator.”

“It all sounds perfectly horrid,” Eden said disdainfully. “Anyway, how could imprisonment of us and the other Sensors in the Vacuum, enable the Murks to take over the world?” it seemed too incredible to Eden.

“Because,” Muffins began, “if you make people unhappy enough, they just stop fighting and give up. That's what the Murks want.”

It was too horrible for Eden to take in all at once. She needed to change the subject, even if it was only for a while.

“Do our keys really fit your briefcase?” she asked.

“Try them,” Muffins offered. “Yours is the one on the left Miss Eden and Mr Fin’s, the one on the right.”

“Oh please don’t call us Miss and Mister, Muffins. It just doesn’t seem right,” Eden implored.

“Very well Miss, I mean Eden,” Muffins corrected himself.

“What's inside?” Fin asked, moving on.

“I can only guess Fin, but probably the secret of who you are, what you must do and how you might get home,” Muffins answered as best he could. “That secret has been locked in my briefcase for thirteen years. I am just the messenger you see.”

Eden tried her key first. It was a perfect fit, the lock clicked and the fastener sprang open. She looked at Fin in disbelief. Fin’s hand was shaking nervously as he inserted his key. Again the lock turned and the fastener released. The briefcase was unlocked and ready to reveal its secrets. Eden opened the lid and looked inside. There were two folders, one pink with Eden's name on it and another that was blue, with Fin’s. Both were tied up with very important looking red ribbon.

“Papers,” she said, “just papers?” Eden looked disappointed.

“No, not *just* papers Eden,” Muffins assured her. “They will be the answers to your questions, or maybe even questions that you haven't asked yet.”

Muffins looked nervously at the people around them.

“I must go,” he said, all of a sudden. “I have already stayed too long and it is dangerous for us to be seen together.”

“Why?” Eden asked, disappointed that the strange little man was leaving.

“Read your folders and then you will understand,” Muffins urged.

He stood, snapped the briefcase shut and touched the brim of his hat.

“I bid you farewell and safe passage. It has been a pleasure meeting you,” Muffins was about to walk away, then added as an afterthought. “Oh, and don't lose those necklaces, they are lucky charms and might keep you safe.”

With that, Muffins was gone. Eden turned to Fin.

“I didn't much like the words *might keep you safe*, Fin,” she whispered, “particularly the *might*.”

Chapter 3

Battersea, London. The next day.

Eden hardly slept at all that night, waiting for dawn to break. Mrs Jones had a strict regime of lights out by eight o'clock in the evening and had installed an automatic timer switch to make sure of it. She couldn't bear the thought of the children having even one extra second of light.

Eden was simply dying to read her folder, even though the thought of it scared her. Sunrise just couldn't come soon enough for her. At last, the first rays of the sun flooded into her room. Eden took a deep breath and untied the red ribbon that held her folder shut. She pulled out the documents with great trepidation.

There was a handwritten letter that began, "*Dearest, darling Eden,*" and five pocket-sized envelopes, numbered one through five. Those three words were enough to start the tears flowing down Eden's face. For no particular reason, Eden put the five little envelopes back in the pink folder. It was as if they were precious beyond measure and needed to be protected. Eden wiped a tear from her cheek and began to read the ornately scrolled writing.

"Dearest, darling Eden,

I have little time to tell you what I must, as it is not safe where I am. Although you are a baby beside me now, you will be thirteen when you read my letter and gone from me those thirteen years. I wrote this never knowing if you would ever read it. I pray that you do and that you are safe. I must assume that you are and that Muffins finds you, because I cannot bear to think otherwise.

You will be wondering who I am and why you are all alone in the world. The 'who' is easy but painful for me; I am your mother and my name is Kikki. The 'why', is not so easy to explain. You will have five numbered envelopes. You must trust me that, when the time comes, you will know when to open each and that they will guide you to me.

From when you read this you will have but three years to find me Eden, or it will be too late for us all. Until then, Muffins will continue to watch over and advise you. I love you Eden and I always will, whatever happens.

Your absent mother,

Kikki x

Eden kissed the letter fondly and placed it back on the table. For the first time in her life she had hope, but she sobbed her heart out nonetheless. The words' "*whatever happens,*" didn't help in the slightest. A superstitious shiver ran up Eden's back, into her neck, leaving her charged with expectation.

It took Eden almost an hour to regain her sensibility. The shock of what she had read had almost paralysed her mind. She read the letter again and then again, looking for some hidden meaning or a clue of how to begin her quest to find her mother. Nothing came immediately to mind. Her brain was still too numb. On the fourth read, it began to make sense.

"I have little time to tell you what I must, as it is not safe where I am," Eden considered her mother's statement carefully.

It could only mean that her mother was writing the letter in a hurry and that she, or *they,* were in danger from the Murks.

"I was with her at the time, as a baby," Eden realised in wonderment, "and Muffins too, ready to take me away, I suppose."

She read on.

"You have but three years to find me Eden or it will be too late for us all," Eden considered that statement too.

"I'm thirteen, so in three years I will be sixteen," Eden could see the relevance of it. "Muffins said we would be safe from the Murks until we were sixteen, by decree of the Creator. He said it would be a mortal sin for them to harm us before then. That is why Mother said it would be *too late* after three years."

Eden opened the pink folder again and laid out the five envelopes in a line. She touched each, as if she might sense what was written inside. Eden picked up number one and ran her thumbnail under the sticky fold, raising it only slightly before putting it down again as if it was red hot.

"No," she said to herself. "Mother said that I would know when it was right to open each of the letters, and it doesn't feel right just now."

Eden was left with only one option. Her mother had said that, "*Muffins would continue to watch over them,*" now she just had to get to Fin and find Muffins!

Chapter 4

Battersea, London. One week later.

It had been the longest week of Eden's life, waiting for a chance to escape unnoticed from the orphanage. Mrs Jones had increased the security. It was as if she knew that something was going on.

"But how could she?" Eden wondered.

The locksmith had replaced all the locks on the doors and windows, with heavy duty ones and big brass bolts too. The orphanage had become even more of a prison and Eden couldn't get out. She couldn't ask Phoebe or Lucy for help either. That would have got them into deep trouble with Mrs Jones. Eden was resourceful though and she had an idea.

The red-bricked orphanage was old and decayed. The strongest part about the windows, were the new locks. The window frames themselves were rotten and the glass was fixed the old fashioned way, with putty. During the afternoon, Eden had gone to the window in her bedroom and scraped the putty away from one of the glass panes with a butter knife. Now, it was only held in place with chewing gum. It had become her personal doorway to freedom.

Eden waited until lights out at eight o'clock, and then carefully pushed out the glass. She was already dressed and ready to go. Earlier in the week, in preparation, she had innocently asked Lucy where Fin lived. The answer she had given, plus Eden reading her mind, was enough.

Eden put the five little envelopes in her pocket, stepped out through the window and slipped silently down the drainpipe to the garden below. She turned around and got the biggest fright of her life.

"Fin!" she exclaimed. "You scared the life out of me."

"I've waited a week to talk to you Eden and I just couldn't wait any longer," Fin said with a boyish shrug.

"Not here! It's not safe," Eden warned. "We have to get to McDonald's."

"McDonald's?" Fin asked, looking puzzled. He couldn't see why.

"Yes," Eden urged, "I'm sure that Muffins will be there waiting for us."

"But why would he be; how can you know that?" Fin asked, looking surprised.

"I just know somehow. I can't explain," Eden said, with much more hope than confidence. "We need to go there Fin; quickly!"

With that, they left the garden and made their way to the cobbled lane that led to the shopping precinct and McDonald's. Although it was only a fifteen minute taxi ride, on foot it was nearly an hour's run for them. They arrived breathless, but even more so when they saw Muffins sat at one of the tables outside, smiling at them expectantly.

"Muffins!" they both gasped at the surprise of it.

He stood, bowed and waved them over to sit with him. The table was laid with two trays of food, both piping hot. There were chicken nuggets and chips for Eden and cheeseburger and chips for Fin. Their favourites! After hugged greetings, Eden pointed at the hot food.

"How did you know we were coming here, and right now Muffins?"

"Exactly the same way that you knew that I would be here Eden," Muffins said. "We can read minds, even from a distance. It's part of our magic, you see."

Muffins twirled his moustache between his fingers and his eyes sparkled with mischief. He looked at the open mouthed and disbelieving children in front of him and chuckled.

"Surely, you have already noticed that you are *different* from the other children, have you not?" Muffins challenged. "Perhaps knowing what happens next, and then it does. Knowing what people are thinking and *moving* things around without touching them."

Eden and Fin looked at each other and nodded. It was true. Muffins continued.

"That's only the beginning of it and why the Murks are afraid of you," Muffins began. "If they don't crush us soon and allow people like you and Fin to develop and find the powers within you, then they are finished and they know it."

Muffins became deadly serious. He looked around for any suspicious people before he continued.

"You will have read your letters and both of you have five envelopes to open when the time is right. You must obey each of them. Failure to do so will be a disaster for all of us. You cannot fail in your quest. You cannot."

Muffins became distracted by the two suspicious looking men that had just arrive. They were wearing dark raincoats with their collars rolled up, and big brimmed hats that obscured their faces.

Muffins looked them up and down. They were Murks, he was sure of it.

"I h-have to go," he stuttered. "Open your first envelope and learn who you are. The orphanage is the passage; you will find what you are looking for there. We will meet again," Muffins said, all in a fluster.

With that, he picked up his cane and scurried off. The two strange men looked undecided for a moment, as if torn between decisions. Much to Eden's and Fin's relief, both men hurried off after Muffins.

The food in front of them suddenly looked much less exciting. Both had lost their appetites and pushed their trays away. After some time, Eden asked the question.

"What do you make of that Fin?"

"Murks," he said, shrugging his shoulders in that typical teenage boy way. "They must have been Murks."

"That's what I thought," Eden agreed. "I hope Muffins is safe."

"I am," Muffins confirmed. He was somehow sat next to them again.

"But how?" Eden asked.

"I left them following an old lady, believing that it was me. We can do these things you see, get into their minds and all that," Muffins added in matter of fact fashion. "Murks are dangerous, but not very bright, you see."

"Are we safe Muffins?" Fin asked.

"For now, yes," Muffins reassured, "but we don't have long before they realise they've been fooled and return. What did your letter say Fin," he asked changing the subject.

"It was from my mother, Kikki. She said that she was not safe and that she loved me," Fin looked like he was at the point of crying, but continued bravely. "She said that the five envelopes would lead me to her and that I only have two years to find her, before it's too late for all of us."

Muffins nodded, and then questioned Eden.

"And yours?"

Eden was clearly in shock at what she had just heard from Fin. Her words were not coming easily.

"M-mine was from Kikki t-too. Only I have th-three years," her eyes were fixed on Fin. She shook her head in disbelief. "That means that you are my brother Fin."

“Quite so,” the strange little man confirmed, “and you have three years, not two, because you will be sixteen a year later than Fin, a year longer, before the Murks are a real danger to you.”

“Hello little sister,” Fin said in wonderment, as he realised the enormity of the situation.

He cupped Eden's hand with his, without any embarrassment.

“I can't tell you how good it feels to know that I'm not alone in the world anymore.”

“Me too Fin. It's awesome.”

Eden looked a little emotional and left it at that. She couldn't trust herself not to cry, so she simply threw her arms around Fin.

Something suddenly occurred to Eden that didn’t seem quite right.

“Muffins,” she asked. “If Fin is my brother, then why doesn’t he smell of roses too?”

It was a good question but Muffins was ready with the answer.

“Your mother, the Queen married into another Royal Family,” Muffins rolled the ends of his magnificent moustache as he explained. “Your father, the King, came from a family with the fragrance of sweets. Finley naturally took after his father in that respect.”

It made sense to Eden. Muffins continued from where Eden had distracted him with her question.

“But why should you wait even two years before you determine your future?” Muffins asked with a mischievous grin. “You could begin your quest today. Right now in fact, if you open your first envelopes.”

Eden and Fin didn't really need any encouragement. They were both dying to know what was in them. Eden reached in her pocket and took out the envelope with the number one on it and Fin did the same. They opened them together and laid them on the table.

“They're exactly the same, apart from mine says, *Darling Eden*, and yours says *Darling Fin*,” Eden noted. “Why would that be Muffins?”

“Because your Mother had no way of knowing if you would both ever meet or even make it to sixteen. Let alone survive the quest,” he added solemnly. “She had to hope that at least one of you would, or there would be no way back for her, or her people.”

"No way back from where?” Fin asked and shivered at the very thought of it.

“From the Vacuum, that’s where the Murks put your mother, just after she wrote Eden's letter. Read on, perhaps that will help,” Muffins suggested.

Eden picked up her letter and read for them.

"Darling Eden,

If the Creator is kind, Muffins will have got you safely to the 'Battersea Home for Children', where you can find your way back to me when the time is right. There are two doors there, in secret places. One is the gateway that will take you nearer to me and the other will take you away from me for ever. That door leads to the Underworld, a place of eternal pain and misery, you must choose carefully.

Muffins will have told you that you are being watched by people we call the 'Murks'. They will try to stop you coming to me at any cost, short of killing you, but there are worse things that they can do to you than take your life. I fear for you. Do not fall into their hands!

Take your envelopes with you. Once you are through the door that leads to me, open your second envelope.

I pray every day for your safety. Be sure that I love you more than life itself.

Your devoted mother,

Kikki."

Eden folded the letter up, kissed it and placed it back in its envelope. Fin did the same.

“What do you make of that, Muffins?” Eden asked, frowning heavily.

“Why Eden, it means that your quest to find your mother, Queen Kikki, has begun,” he twisted the ends of his moustache between his fingers in that way of his and grinned.

“Queen Kikki? Eden and Fin asked in unison, shocked at Muffin’s statement.

“Yes. Kikki, Queen of Paradise. All will become clear in due course,” Muffins was dismissive about it. “More importantly, you now know that the gateway into her world is somewhere in the orphanage. You only have to find out where.”

It was the most exciting thought, but scary too.

“I will look for it tomorrow night, after lights out,” Eden said bravely.

A sudden feeling of dread came over her and she turned hopefully to Fin.

“Could you come to me after eight o’clock tomorrow night? We could look for it together. I would feel much safer that way.”

Eden blushed at her little plea for help. The smile that Fin returned was much braver than he felt.

“We are in this together little Princess. You can count on me.”

Eden could sense that Muffins was agitated and needed to leave again. She had one more question though and it just couldn't wait.

“Mother never mentions anything about our father,” Eden began, “and nor do you. Why?”

Muffins expression was grave. He was clearly uncomfortable with what he was about to say.

“Your father, the King, is lost Eden along with so many other fathers.”

Muffins appeared to have aged in the telling of it.

“They learned that the Murks had taken over the orphanages in this world and tried to come to save you all. It was futile though. Your Mother wrote those letters after he disappeared.”

“Lost? Disappeared? But how and where?”

Tears were already flowing down Eden's face, even though she had never met her father. She was crying for the loss of him, the loss of the man that she had never known.”

"Shortly after I took you to the Battersea Home for Children Eden, your father found out that the Murks had taken over the orphanage. He and other fathers tried to come to rescue their children."

Muffins stopped. It was too terrible to say to such young children.

"Go on Muffins, we need to know everything," Eden encouraged and Muffins continued.

"The Murks found out and laid a trap for them. They changed the appearance of the gateways to trick them. Instead of taking the one that led to this world and you, they took the other gateway that your mother warned you of in her letter. They went to that place of eternal pain and damnation, the Underworld."

Eden and Fin clung to each other for comfort, sharing the pain that they both felt. It took some time before Fin could trust his voice.

"Is there any way back from this place of eternal damnation?"

"Only the Creator can undo things that have been done," Muffins said soulfully, "only the Creator."

Eden and Fin looked deep into each other's eyes. There was no need for words, because they could share thoughts.

"Yes Fin, we will find the Creator somehow and bring him back and Mother too," Eden agreed. "I don't know how but we will. We must!"

Chapter 5

Battersea, London. The next day.

It had been another painfully long day for Eden, waiting for lights out. She had spent the time with Phoebe, asking random questions about the orphanage. Although she had been there for thirteen years, Eden had no idea of life outside of her living quarters. She had not been permitted to roam free. Phoebe had drawn a picture of the layout of the orphanage that Eden had immediately committed to memory; every last detail of it.

The red-bricked orphanage was set out like an old castle. Four terraces of buildings, set in a square, like a mews, enclosed a courtyard. They were like castle walls and where the children and staff lived. At the centre of the courtyard, was a stone tower that was much, much older than the rest of the orphanage. It had no windows, other than slits in the stonework for bows and arrows, and a single, massive solid oak door. This was a fortress, like the keep of a castle and where Mrs Jones lived, alone.

Phoebe had told her that even Mrs Jones's tower was plunged into darkness, when the automatic timer turned the electricity off at eight o'clock at night.

"I will need a torch," Eden had decided and took one from the kitchen.

She was already convinced that the gateway would be somewhere inside that tower, guarded by the evil Mrs Jones. Eden was also convinced that the only door in, would be locked and she had no idea how they might get in. On that score, she was hoping for inspiration, when the time came.

At last, it was seven-thirty and time for Eden to say goodnight to Phoebe and Lucy. Eden's goodnights were far too earnest and final, which caused great concern to her loving foster parents. It took some time before Eden had convinced them that she was OK. The problem was that Eden had experienced one of her premonitions. Somehow she knew that she wasn't coming back, one way or another. It was sad and she wondered how they would cope with not knowing what happened to her, whatever that might be.

Eden had already chosen what she would wear and it was all laid out on her bed in readiness.

"Something practical," she had decided, as she might need to run. "Away from something probably," Eden conceded and shuddered at the very thought of it.

That meant dresses, skirts and sandals were out! Eden put on her jeans, t-shirt, jumper and boots, pulled her long blonde hair back in a ponytail and tied the torch around her neck with a shoelace.

She took one final look at herself in the mirror. Eden was hoping to see a warrior looking back at her, but all she saw was a frightened little schoolgirl.

Eden took a deep breath to steel herself, and then took the glass out of the window. She waited for the painful seconds to pass, before the automatic switch tripped. At last it did and the room fell into darkness. Eden stepped out, reached for the drainpipe and slid down to the lawn and her waiting brother.

“Fin! You look as white as a ghost,” Eden was quite taken aback by it.

“I always look like this. It's my colour,” he said defensively. “It's not like I'm afraid, or anything.”

“Good,” Eden felt reassured, “because I'm petrified.”

Fin put on his bravest smile, but it was all bravado and they both knew it. They naturally held hands to give themselves strength.

“I know where the gateway is,” Eden whispered, with more confidence than she actually had. “There’s a tower in the courtyard. It's much more than a thousand years old and it's where Mrs Jones lives. It has to be there, Fin.”

“I remember it. We all thought it was haunted,” Fin added, much to Eden’s annoyance.

"Great Fin; that's just what I needed to know right now," she looked even more scared now.

"It probably isn't," Fin added, but it was already too late.

"*Probably* Fin? How about it's *definitely* not haunted?"

Eden didn't want to dwell on the thought of ghosts; it was enough to have Murks on her mind. She changed the subject.

"It's going to be dark in there Fin, so I've brought a torch," Eden said, proud of her foresight.

"Me too," Fin switched it on under his chin, grinning devilishly with his tongue hanging out to the side.

"Great!" Eden said sarcastically. "Something else I really don't need, Devils."

Eden recalled the map in her head and navigated them through the bushes to the tower that was Mrs Jones's house. She wasn't prepared for quite how massive it was. It really was a veritable fortress and looked impregnable. It was circular and the stone walls went up fifteen metres. The lowest of the slits in the stonework, for shooting arrows from, was five metres above the ground and not even wide enough to put your head through. The solid oak door was black with age and would have needed a battering ram to break it down. Eden tried the big iron door knob in hope, but even with all her strength, it didn't budge. Not even a bit.

Eden and Fin both felt vulnerable, stood there out in the open. They huddled together against the stone wall while they thought about it.

“We are so close Fin, so close. We have to get in; it just can't end here. Mother is counting on us,” Eden felt like crying at the impossibility of it.

“What was it that Muffins said to us?” Fin asked. It was as if to jog his own memory and help him think, more than a question. “Wasn’t it something about the Murks having to crush people like us, before we discover our powers and that they would be finished if we do?”

“Yes, that's exactly what Muffins said Fin. Exactly. But he never went on to say what they were.”

“We have to find them Eden, but I can't imagine what they might be,” Fin lamented.

They crouched there for several minutes wondering what they might do. It was hopeless. Eden broke the silence.

“I wonder what it’s like inside,” she whispered.

Fin turned to reply, but Eden was gone. Disappeared! He looked all around, scared that he would be taken too. He waited and waited, expecting to get grabbed, but there was nothing and nobody there. Fin made himself as small as possible, pressing himself between the stone wall and the ground, waiting for something to happen. After a long moment, there was a loud click. The big iron door knob began to turn with a ghostly groan and the door creaked open. Fin was petrified, squashed there against the wall, waiting for the Murks to come out.

“Eden,” he gasped, as she peered around the open door.

“Quickly Fin, come inside!”

She beckoned him to enter. Fin was up on his feet and inside in a flash. Eden closed the door as silently as she could behind them. They stood there in the darkness with just Eden's torch shining on their faces.

“How did you get in?” Fin blurted and Eden immediately hushed him.

“Shh, be quiet Fin, we don't know where Mrs Jones is.”

“But how?” he whispered.

“I don't know Fin, I just wondered what it would be like to be inside the fortress, and then somehow I was.”

“That must be one of those powers that Muffins talked about, our imagination,” Fin deduced. “Awesome!”

“We must be quiet and search for the gateway,” Eden urged. “Don't talk to me, use your thoughts.”

Fin nodded. They walked cautiously into the cavernous darkness of the building, with no idea of where they were going. After about twenty steps, they came to a staircase. The flights of stairs went up and down.

"Which way?" Fin asked in his thoughts.

"Down first," Eden decided. "I think Mrs Jones is more likely to live and sleep upstairs."

Fin agreed and so they took the stairs leading down. There was a pungent smell of dampness, rotting wood and something else that they had never smelt before. It smelt like death. The torch lights cast long shadows that flicked across the stone walls, like demons following them down to Hell. It was the creepiest feeling ever. They held hands tightly, as if it would protect them from something evil.

When they reached the bottom, they came to a cellar that had nothing in it and seemed to go on forever. Wherever they shone their torches, the light just disappeared as if into eternity. They walked on holding hands into the darkness, always scared that there was something behind them. Eden stopped and shared her thoughts with Fin.

"If we keep going, we may never find our way back to the stairs Fin. We need to leave a trail, like Hansel and Gretel did in the forest, but I haven't got anything to drop."

"I've got a packet of lemon sherbets," Fin said reluctantly and dropped one of his precious sweets on the floor. It rattled on the stone flags.

They continued for some time, with Fin mournfully dropping sweets as they went.

"I've only got three left Eden, we can't go much further."

It was true. If they got lost and their batteries ran out, they could be there forever.

"We have to go to the last sweet and then a bit further Fin, for Mum."

It was the first time that Eden had ever said the word *Mum* and it brought a lump to her throat.

"For you Mum," she whispered as they pressed on into the darkness.

"Last one," Fin thought out loud, as he dropped it on the floor. It landed with a thud, not the usual rattle that it did on the stone flags.

They stopped in their tracks and pointed their torches downwards. To their surprise, they were stood on top of a black wooden trapdoor, with a big lock on it. Fin tried the door, but it was no good. It was locked fast.

"I wish our little golden keys fitted this, but they are much too small," Eden lamented.

She touched the chain around her neck regretfully as she passed her thoughts to Fin.

"Oh my God Fin," Eden said out loud and regretted it immediately. "My key, it's huge!"

Eden reached inside her t-shirt and took off her necklace. The golden key was ten times bigger than when it had opened Muffins' briefcase. She placed it in the lock and twisted it. The old rusty lock opened reluctantly. Their hearts were racing as Fin slowly lifted the trapdoor.

The stench of something rotting hit them immediately and rocked them backwards. Screams and howls of agony and despair bellowed out from the open door. It was like they had opened the gateway to Hell.

"Shut it Fin! Shut it!" Eden screamed at the top of her voice. "It's the wrong gateway!"

Fin slammed the trapdoor shut in nothing short of panic. They both stood on it as Fin fumbled with the lock. They could hear the howls and scratching of fingernails on the wood below their feet. At last, the golden key turned with a reassuring click and they jumped backwards from it. They were safe. Well at least for now.

"The gateway we want must be upstairs Fin. Quickly, follow the sweets back to the stairs," Eden said, using her thoughts again, instead of her voice. "I hope Mrs Jones didn't hear me scream out," she added and crossed her fingers superstitiously.

Mrs Jones was a creature better suited to the night. She only needed a glimmer of light to see, and what she couldn't see, she could smell!

"Brats," she muttered as the lights went out. "That will keep them quiet till morning."

She cursed the Murks for giving her the job of keeping a watchful eye over earthly children and Sensors. She hated them all, particularly the Sensors. Mrs Jones comforted herself with the thought that it was only for three more years before she could condemn Eden, the last of her charges, to the Vacuum. Then be free of her. Free of Sensors and free of the orphanage.

Mrs Jones made herself a cup of pungent black coffee and took it to her room on the first floor of the tower. Mrs Jones sipped it through her thin lips, while she plotted about how she would spoil the next day for everyone at the orphanage. She was almost asleep when she heard someone cry out in fear. The scream had come from somewhere downstairs. She flew out of bed and was on the landing in moments.

Fin quickly followed the sweet trail that led them back to the stairs. It took all his effort not to pick the sweets up though, as they were his passion. Their hearts were beating hard with fright and the exertion of the run back to the stairs. At last, their torches picked up the staircase in the distance. With a big sigh of relief, they turned into it and took the first flight upwards, away from the horror that was behind them. That was when they came face to face with the evil Mrs Jones!

“Run!” Eden screamed. “Follow the sweets back again!”

They turned on their heels and fled back towards the trapdoor and that terrible place below it. Fin could read Eden's thoughts and knew what she was planning. He just prayed that it would work.

“You can't escape, there’s no way out!” they heard Mrs Jones scream after them, as they ran down the path of sweets.

“Turn your torch off Eden, it will slow Mrs Jones down, I can smell the sweets,” Fin assured her.

It was amazing. Fin ran unerringly on through the blackness, led only by the sweet scent. Holding Eden's hand, he guided her to the trapdoor. Mrs Jones was in rage, ranting and cursing behind them. They were gaining distance though. With her free hand, Eden took her necklace off and held her golden key at the ready. The moment that their feet hit the wooden trapdoor, Eden fell to her knees. Thankfully, she found the lock quickly and opened it.

“Wait Fin. Wait until she is right on us, then help me throw the door open.”

They waited in terror as Mrs Jones’s flat feet slammed against the stone floor getting ever closer. She was still shouting abuse as she ran, which helped them place her, even in the blackness. Eden needed to make sure that Mrs Jones found them on the run. She screamed out to help Mrs Jones find her way straight to them.

“You will never find us you evil old witch!”

It was enough, Mrs Jones could place them in the dark exactly and she ran even faster.

“Now Fin, now!” Eden yelled and they threw the trapdoor open.

Mrs Jones’s feet suddenly found mid-air, as she plunged down into that hellish place. Her blood-curdling screams were deafening as they slammed the trapdoor shut and locked it. They stepped back to what seemed a safe distance and held each other in fear and dread.

“Take me out of here Fin, I just can't bear it,” Eden was close to freaking out and only just held herself together.

Fin led them back to the stairs, following the smell of the sweets. Once again he resisted the temptation to pick them up. By the time they climbed the stairs up to the ground floor, their torches were just a glimmer.

"Old batteries," Fin said, shrugging his shoulders. "I can't see a thing now."

"Me either," Eden agreed, feeling the snake of fear curling in her stomach. "We need to wait until morning until the lights come back on."

It felt cold as the grave in the tower. They huddled together by the massive front door for warmth and comfort.

"We'll sleep one at a time, while the other watches out for ghosts," Eden said with a tremble in her voice. "Or Devils," she added and shuddered at the thought of it.

"There aren't any," Fin assured her. "I was only kidding."

"Were you Fin? How can you be so sure after what we just saw?" Eden was far from convinced. "Anyway, there could be Murks. We will sleep one at a time or not at all Fin. OK?"

"OK, you sleep first then Eden. I'll stand guard," he said bravely, but quite how you stand guard over *ghosts, Devils and Murks*, Fin wasn't quite sure.

They had been left exhausted by the terror of what had just happened to them. Eden fell asleep quickly leaving Fin battling against his tiredness and dread, right up until the early hours of the morning. Every little noise seemed deafening to him, amplified by his fear and anxiety. Even the rats that passed by from time to time sniffing at them seemed to have hobnail boots on. Fin was immensely relieved when Eden woke.

“It’s my turn to stand guard Fin. Have you seen or heard anything?”

No, was the answer she was hoping for.

“Just some rats,” Fin said honestly, “but they are just being nosey, I think.”

“Go to sleep Fin,” Eden replied, slightly offishly. And then said to herself. “You *think*? Great Fin, that’s just great...”

There was a loud click and all the lights went on. It briefly crossed Eden's mind that Mrs Jones had met her fate through denying the orphanage electricity. If there were lights in the cellar, she never would have fallen into their trap.

“Poetic justice,” she thought and shook Fin.

“Fin, wake up. It's morning.”

He woke with a start and looked around, not knowing where he was for a moment. When his mind cleared, the first thing he thought of was food.

“I'm hungry,” Fin declared. “Can we go back down and get my sweets?”

Eden was wide-mouthed in shock at the very suggestion suggestion.

“I'm not going down there ever again Fin. You can...”

It was too late. Fin was already grinning at her. Eden had been well and truly *got.* Fin had no intention of going down there either. Not ever again!

“Ha, ha; very funny Fin,” Eden said wryly. “There might be some food upstairs though. Shall we go and see?”

It was much easier to be brave now that there was light and that Mrs Jones was gone. They found the kitchen on the first floor. It had a stone sink and a stone worktop. A stone table with stone stools was set in the centre of the stone floor. Everything was stone. Even the stale bread felt and tasted like stone, but they devoured it nonetheless.

“Shall we start at the top and work down?” Eden offered. “Only I imagine that the gateway we are looking for is likely to be at the top, as the other, was at the bottom.”

It seemed logical, so they climbed the stairs up to the roof. When they got there, they found themselves in another empty stone room apart from a ladder set against the wall.

“Nothing,” Fin groaned in disappointment. “It's just an empty room with a ladder that goes nowhere.”

Fin's disappointment was profound. His shoulders were slumped and he kicked the floor petulantly. He turned to face Eden expecting to see her just as broken, but she was looking up at the ceiling with just the biggest smile on her face, ever.

“Eden?” he questioned, looking puzzled.

“Look Fin. Look up!”

Above them, was a golden door in the ceiling that was nothing like the black one in the cellar.

“That's the gateway to our mother. She's waiting for us Fin. She's waiting behind that golden door!”

Fin’s hand went automatically to his necklace. He felt the heavy weight of the key that now hung there and smiled at Eden.

“I have the key,” he whispered, then shouted. “I have the key!”

Fin dragged the ladder to the trapdoor and was up it trying the key in a moment.

“It fits Eden, it fits!”

The lock turned with ease, not reluctantly like the rusted one in the cellar.

"Wait for me Fin!" Eden shouted.

She hurried up the ladder until she was stood beside him on the same rung. Their excitement was boiling over. It was a delicious mixture of anticipation and fear.

"It pushes upwards Eden, help me."

They pushed and it gave a little. A slither of brilliant sunshine, burst through the crack and lit up their expectant faces.

"Push harder!" Fin urged.

They put all their strength behind the door and it flew open. Eden and Fin found themselves looking up into a green sky with yellow fluffy clouds.

"Together?" Eden asked, her voice shaking with a delicious mixture of excitement and fear.

"Together princess," Fin confirmed.

They took a deep breath and stepped through the trapdoor into another world.

Chapter 6

Paradise, moments later.

Eden and Fin looked around in wonderment. They were in a world unlike anything they could ever have imagined. Everywhere they looked, was a riot of colour. The grass around them was blue, like the ocean, as were the leaves on the red trees. It seemed everything that was green in their world, was blue in this one and everything blue was green.

The air was perfumed with every smell you could think of. Some of the smells were nostalgic, from their early childhood. Some were either forgotten until now, or just gone. Eden wondered whether her and Fin's smells would disappear on Earth, if anything ever happened to them.

It was a horrible thought and she knew that Fin had shared it too. It seemed that here, in this other world, that her mental bond with Fin was absolute. There was no longer any need for words as they shared minds. Fin felt it too. They both needed to distract themselves from the enormity of it and decided to stick with the comfort of words. Just for a while, at least.

"This is awesome Fin. Look at those birds. They are like birds of Paradise, so beautiful and they keep changing colour too."

"That's because they are Chameleon birds," the gruff voice from behind them said. "And they are birds of Paradise, because this *is* Paradise."

Eden and Fin turned around, startled by the strange voice. It was a dog. A talking dog! Eden looked around her for any other explanation, but there was none. They were alone, other than the little black, curly haired dog.

"Um, excuse me but," Eden addressed the dog and immediately felt completely ridiculous for doing so. She struggled to continue, "You didn't just say something, did you?"

It was as stupid as asking a tree for an opinion on autumn, *so* stupid.

"Ruff-ruff!" was the dog's immediate response.

Eden looked at Fin, waiting for him to make a joke of it. What happened next blew them both away.

"My name's Rags," the dog announced, "and you are?" he prompted.

Eden looked at Fin in disbelief. It hung in the balance for a while, and then they burst out laughing.

"And why not," Fin chuckled, "everything else is impossible!"

"Ruff," Rags began. "You do have names, don't you? We do here, only we are not so strange as you."

If a dog could have a quizzical look, Rags did. Eden rescued the situation.

"Rags, we are so pleased to meet you, but it's just that, well..."

"It's just that I'm a dog and you are Sensors exiled to Earth," Rags interrupted. "We talk where you have come from too; it's just that you don't listen to us there. But I know that you mean well," he added and grinned, somehow.

It was a gentle rebuke. They were clearly going to be friends.

"How do you know that we are Sensors from Earth?" Eden asked.

"Muffins said that you were coming," Rags muttered distractedly.

He was more interested in sniffing the grass around one of the red trees that strangely had two old rusted tins of paint next to it. One was gold and the other, black. There were paintbrushes on top of them that had gone hard over time.

"Muffins, Rags?" Fin asked. "You know Muffins?"

"Every man and his dog, knows Muffins," Rags yapped, and ran off after the little purple mouse that he had disturbed.

Eden and Fin were completely at a loss. This was just too fantastic for words. Eden was the first to find her wits.

"Muffins must have been here then," Eden shook her head as she tried to fathom it out. "But how and when?"

"And why didn't he just bring us with him then?" Fin added, scratching his head. It was a conundrum.

"I think this is about us Fin. Somehow I know that we have to do this alone and we have to earn it."

"I think it's time we opened letter number two from Mum," Fin suggested. "But first, I think we should lock the gateway that we came through. We don't know who might follow us."

As Fin locked it, he noticed that the golden door had the weathered remains of black paint on it.
"Why would anyone paint a gold door black in the middle of the country," he wondered.

Eden picked up his thoughts.

"And why would someone paint this black door gold?" Eden asked.

She was stood by another trapdoor only a few steps away. It dawned on both of them at the same time.

"This is where the Murks tricked our father and the other men of Paradise to go through the wrong gateway," Fin knew that he was right. "It was a trap. Dad must have walked straight into it and straight into the Underworld."

It was all beginning to seem real to them now and it was emotional. They held each other for a while, realising what their father must have gone through to try to save them.

"We will make it all right again Eden. We must, somehow. Open the letter."

Eden took the crumpled envelope from her pocket. Her hands were shaking as she opened it. She swallowed deeply and began to read the letter.

"Darling Eden,

If you have opened this second letter, it means that you have arrived safely in Paradise. For that, I thank the Creator, but you are not safe. You must be careful and vigilant at all times. Here, things are not always as they seem. There are many illusions and the Murks' corruption is everywhere.

You have far to travel to get to me. First, you must find the Crystal Maze. In the middle of the maze are two more gateways with gate masters. They are brothers. One will always tell you the truth and the other will always lie. Choose which gate you go through carefully, as one will take you closer to me and the other, closer to your father. If you choose the wrong one, we will never be together Eden; ever.

Trust your instincts Eden, always.

Your devoted mother,

Kikki."

The letter left them both sad. The thought of where their father was, brought back the sound of those agonised screams coming from the cellar at Mrs Jones's tower. They realised that their father's screams would also be part of that cacophony. Eden broke that painful silence.

"We will find him Fin, before this is over and set him free, or die trying. Do you agree?"

"Agreed," Fin declared. His chin was jutted out in defiance.

They gave each other their bravest faces and shook hands on it. Both were terrified at the thought though. Rags came running back with his little pink tongue hanging out of his black face. He was panting with the exertion of the chase. Somehow, he was frowning, looking a little miffed. He yapped his disappointment.

"I must be getting old," he conceded gruffly. "Those little critters are either getting quicker, or I'm getting slower. It's lucky I don't depend on them for food."

Quite strangely, Rags began eating from a silver bowl that appeared in front of him out of nowhere. It was full of meat and gravy.

"Where did that come from?" Eden asked. "It wasn't there just now."

"I just imagined it. That's how it works here," Rags said between mouthfuls.

He *imagined* two more silver bowls of meat and gravy.

"Would you like to join me?" Rags grunted as he snaffled the food from his bowl.

It was all Eden and Fin could do not to laugh at the thought of them eating from dog bowls.

"No, Rags. We have only just eaten," Fin lied, kindly. "But you go ahead, please."

Rags did, and devoured all three. When Rags was finished, Eden asked her question.

"How do we get to the Crystal Maze, Rags?"

Rags growled. It was a growl that a dog does when it senses danger.

"Not many come back from the Crystal Maze," Rags had become nervous. "Murks, you see. They are everywhere."

"Will you take us Rags?" Eden asked. "We have a quest, a destiny to fulfil. We don't have a choice."

Rags thought on it while, had a good scratch, growled grumpily and then conceded.

“Very well,” he yapped, “but don’t say that I didn’t warn you. This way...”

Rags set off proudly at a march with his nose and tail high. He was clearly doing his best to look authoritative. But then the little purple mouse appeared and Rags was off on the chase again, in completely the opposite direction.

“This might take some time,” Eden sighed.

Chapter 7

Paradise. The Crystal Maze.

It was early evening when they reached the Crystal Maze. It really wasn’t very far; it was just that Rags had come across many distractions along the way. Their journey revealed a wonderland of strange animals and plants in every colour of the rainbow. There were fragrances on the journey that they had never encountered before, and sounds that they had never heard.

Eden and Fin were in awe at the diversity of it all and wondered who and where the spirits of those fragrances might be. There would be so many: like she was the spirit of roses, Fin the spirit of sweets and Muffins, the spirit of burnt wood. They wondered if those spirits were still alive, or had been taken by the Murks to the Vacuum. They decided that the spirits would be alive and safe, as those fragrances would be gone already, otherwise.

Rags yapped excitedly, as the vision of the vast Crystal Maze appeared in front of them. The orange of the setting sun reflected of it, making it look like it was on fire. He scampered down the hill, wagging his little black tail enthusiastically. Eden and Fin followed at a full run. Minutes later, the three of them stood breathless at the crystal gates.

“How do we find our way to the centre?” Fin asked, to no one in particular.

There were dozens of glass corridors that seemed to branch off into dozens of others, and mirrors set everywhere that seemed to double the options.

“And how would we ever find our way back?” he added, despairingly.

“We don’t Fin; this is a one way ticket. When we get to the gateways, we go through to wherever it takes us.”

Eden looked determined and it bolstered Fin’s confidence.

“Rags,” Fin began. “Can you smell the gate keepers?”

“Can a dog smell a bone a mile away?” Rags looked insulted and chose to have another good scratch, to leverage his disdain. “Of course I can. I smelt you coming from another world, didn’t I?” he yapped.

Eden knelt down beside Rags and stroked him until the stiffness went out of his little body.

“Would you do us the honour of being our guide Rags?” she asked.

Rags yapped his consent. He put his nose to the ground and sniffed his way, very professionally, through the Crystal gates to one of the corridors. After only minutes, both Eden and Fin knew that they would never find their way out of the maze. They were lost. They just hoped to God that Rags wasn’t.

Eden and Fin followed Rags trustingly, long after the sky had turned black above them. Strangely, the crystal around them glowed eerily with blue light, such that it never got dark. At last, they came to a crystal room in the middle of the maze. Just as their mother had said in her letter, there were two doors facing each other, with two men stood next to them. They were dressed in crystal suits of armour and both carried crystal swords. Rags growled disapprovingly.

“Stop! Who goes there?” the gate keepers called out in unison. “Make yourselves known to us and why you seek entry to the gateways!”

“It’s just as Mum said,” Fin whispered, in awe.

“My name is Eden and this is Fin,” Eden announced with a confidence that she really didn’t feel. “We have come here to find our mother, Queen Kikki of Paradise.”

“Then you need to go through this door,” one of the crystal clad brothers said, standing aside to let them through.

Fin smiled his thanks and began to walk towards the door.

“No it’s this one,” corrected the other brother, also standing aside.

“Stop Fin!” Eden shouted. “He might be lying.”

“But so might the other,” Fin defended. “Anyway, he said it first and probably didn’t have time to think about lying.”

“No Fin, that’s not how it works. That’s like tossing a coin, when your life depends on it.”

“You are allowed to ask us one question, but only one,” offered the first gate keeper. We will tell you the truth as we see it.”

“He’s lying Fin,” Eden was sure of it. “I’ve read about this, years ago. It was about *Knights and Knaves*. The Knights always told the truth and the Knaves always lied. You had to solve puzzles. This was just one of them.”

"What was the answer to the puzzle?" Fin asked, more than just a little impressed.

"Well I think you ask one brother what gate the other brother would tell you was safe, and go through that one." Eden scratched her chin in thought. "Or was it, go through the other one? I'm not sure."

"Great," Fin said sarcastically, "don't you ever pay attention?"

"Shut up Fin, I'm thinking. I'm sure about the question though, but not so sure about the answer."

Eden took a deep breath and addressed one of the brothers.

"If I was to ask your brother, which gate will take us to our mother, the Queen? Which gate would he tell me to go through?"

"That one," the gate keeper said confidently, pointing to his brother's gate.

Eden thought on it for several minutes, running all the possibilities through her head. At last she had made her decision.

"Come on Fin, we are going through this one."

"But he said the *other* one," Fin looked scared and confused.

"Trust me Fin," Eden insisted.

She took his hand and marched him to the gate. Rags followed faithfully. The gate keeper opened the gate, but all they could see through it was mist. They took a giant leap of faith and stepped through.

Chapter 8

Paradise. The Journey.

When the mist cleared, they were stood in bright sunshine again. It seemed most strange to them, as it was dark when they had left the Crystal Maze. Eden and Fin worked out between them that it must have meant that they had either moved in time, or in space. Or even both. The air was warmer too, like a different season. Eden had clearly chosen the right gateway.

“How did you work that out? How did you know which was the safe gateway?” Fin asked, both relieved and seriously impressed.

“Well, Fin. It didn’t matter which brother I asked. If it was the liar, then he would lie about his honest brother’s answer. So we couldn’t go through the gateway he pointed to. If it was the brother who always told the truth, he would know that his brother would lie and point to the wrong gateway. Clear?”

“As mud,” Fin conceded and changed the subject. “Where do you think we are?”

"I don't know Fin. Wherever we are, it's closer to Mum than we were."

"I think we should open the next letter," Fin urged.

"I was just about to," Eden reached for the envelopes in her pocket and selected the one with number three on it. "Here goes."

As Eden opened the envelope, Rags yapped and set off at a pace. He had clearly got the scent of something; something that he found much more interesting than *letters*. Eden began to read.

"Darling Eden,

I have prayed every day that you would open this letter. If you are, then you will have managed to outwit the gate keepers. I hope that one day you will be with me, telling me how you did that. I would be so proud of you.

You still have far to go to get to me Eden and you will need to stay alert. Remember that you have powers within you, yet to explore. Things are not always as they seem and nothing is impossible. When all seems lost, dig deep and find those powers.

Now you must find the Fountain of Enlightenment. Use your imagination and be open to its power and its possibility. The Fountain will open the way to the Creator. Only he can undo all the wrongs of the Murks.

I wish you God's speed.

Your devoted mother,

Kikki."

"The Fountain of Enlightenment; we have to go there, Fin. But where on Earth might that be?" Eden asked looking around her, hoping to see a clue.

"Where in *Paradise*," Fin corrected. "It all looks the same everywhere you turn. There's nothing for miles and nobody to ask."

It was true. They were in the middle of a desert, only the sand was pink here, not dirty yellow. There were purple coloured mountains all around them in the distance. It was like they were in a vast sandy crater.

"Well," Eden began, thoughtfully, "everything in the distance is all the same, whichever way you look. It could take forever to find, the fountain if it's in the mountains. But what if the Fountain of Enlightenment was like an oasis in the middle of desert?"

"Yes, good thinking Eden. Only thing is, it would take a day or two in this baking hot sunshine to walk out across the desert to the middle of it. Then, if it wasn't there and there was no water, it would take another three to walk to the mountains, maybe more. I don't think we would make it that long without water."

It was true, and they both knew it. If they set off deep into the desert and were wrong, they would die of heat exhaustion and thirst on the journey back; definitely.

"We have no choice Fin," Eden lamented.

Using a prominent mountain peak to navigate by, they set off into the shimmering heat of the desert. The sun baked down on them and the air felt hot and dry to breathe. They started off at a brisk pace, chatting as they went, but they soon slowed to a gentle pace and stopped talking to conserve energy. They called out Rag's name every now and again, but there was no sign of him. He had probably got lost after his chase, they decided.

It was several hours later, before they realised that the centre of the desert was very much further away than they had estimated. At the rate they were going, and allowing for sleep, it would probably take another four days to get there. Neither said it in words, but they were both becoming afraid that they wouldn't even make it to the centre of the desert, let alone back. They were desperately thirsty, scared and beginning to hallucinate.

"Fin, I can't go on. Not without a drink anyway," Eden looked desperate. "Can we stop for a while?"

"Just for a few minutes then Eden, but we are dehydrating dangerously. We have to get to a waterhole as soon as we can or..."

Fin cut the sentence short, but they both knew what he was going to say. They sat on the hot sand, lost in their own thoughts, both knowing that they were not going to survive the oppressive heat of the desert without water. Eden broke the glum silence.

"We can't just give up Fin. We have to get to the Fountain of Enlightenment somehow; Mum and Dad's lives depend on it."

Just as Eden began dragging herself to her feet to press on, Rags came bounding up to them. He yapped enthusiastically and Eden fussed him.

"Poor Rags, you must be thirsty too," her tone was sorrowful.

She felt guilty for bringing him to this desolate and hostile place, where they all faced the very real prospect of dying of thirst. Rags yapped his agreement.

"Yes, very thirsty and hungry too, as it happens," he said gruffly, and then added. "Chasing little critters in this heat is hard work, particularly when the little blighters get away."

Eden and Fin watched in awe as Rags lapped water enthusiastically from the silver bowl that had suddenly appeared in front of him.

"Rags," Fin began, "I don't suppose you could conjure up two more bowls of water, could you?"

No sooner said, than two bowls of cool water appeared. Fin and Eden grabbed them and drank thirstily. They were no longer put off from drinking out of a dog's bowl and drained them rapidly. Rags produced two more, and then two more.

"Oh my God, did water ever taste this good?" Eden asked.

"No, never, it's better even than Coca-Cola!" Fin was in ecstasy.

"You prefer Coca-Cola then?" Rags asked. "Hate the stuff myself," he growled disapprovingly, but produced two bottles, nonetheless.

"Rags! You hero!" Fin was thrilled.

They drank, but not so urgently now. Fin was chatting away with Rags and laughing, but Eden had gone quiet. She was deep in thought. Fin noticed the change in her.

"What's the matter Eden, we are safe now."

"Yes we are Fin, but we nearly killed ourselves out of pure stupidity. We are only safe because of Rags."

Eden was disappointed in herself.

"I don't understand why you are looking so glum. Everything is OK, isn't it?" Fin didn't get it.

"Don't you remember Fin that Mum's last letter said we have powers within us, yet to explore, and that things aren't always as they seem? She said that nothing is impossible. She told us that when all seems lost, dig deep and find those powers."

"Yes, I remember, but..." Eden cut him off.

"But we didn't. Pick up Rags Fin, then hold my hand and trust me."

It was the second time that Eden had asked Fin to *trust* her. Fin conceded that she had been right about which gateway to choose at the Crystal Maze. That episode went a long way towards him trusting her again now. Fin took Eden's hand in good faith.

Eden appeared to go into deep, almost trancelike thought. The air around them filled with a static electrical charge that caused Eden's long blonde hair to stand out around her head like a lion's mane in a storm. Everything went out of focus for a long moment and the scenery around them faded away. Moments later, the electrical storm abated. They were now standing holding hands, with Fin carrying Rags, in a completely different place. They were still in the pink desert though, but next to them was a crystal clear pool of water with a fountain gushing up from its depths. The purple coloured mountains were still there, but now they were looking back at them from the very middle of the desert.

“How, I mean, what did you do Eden?” Fin asked in awe.

“I’ve been so stupid Fin. Do you remember how I got into Mrs Jones’s tower?”

“Yes,” Fin confirmed,” you just imagined being in there, and then you were.”

“Exactly Fin, and that’s *exactly* how we got here. Mum and Muffins have said that we are *special*, and we are.”

“A-M-A-Z-I-N-G,” Fin emphasised every letter, “You have probably saved our lives.”

“I think I just did that,” Rags grumbled. “I gave you the water when you needed it,” he pointed out and sneezed in disgust.

“Yes you did Rags, and much more,” Eden praised. “You also gave me the idea to use my imagination!”

Eden fussed Rags, who looked most pleased with himself. Fin put him down, only for Rags to immediately go off on the chase of yet another furry little animal. An orange one this time...

“It will end just the same way,” Fin lamented; “just another disappointment and another bowl of imaginary dog food.”

“It will,” Eden Agreed, “but look, we have found the Fountain of Enlightenment. I wonder what fortune that might bring us, Fin?”

Chapter 9

Paradise. The Fountain of Enlightenment.

Eden and Fin looked around them for inspiration, for *enlightenment*. All there was in front of them was a deep pool and a fountain. That was it, nothing else. It was so disappointing. After some time, Fin looked at the positive side of things.

"At least we will have something real to drink," Fin sighed.

"Do we Fin? Do we really?" Eden was far from convinced. "Is any of this real? Am I in your dream, or are you in mine?"

"Don't you see Fin? This might just all be make believe. None of this might ever have happened. Well not here in *Paradise* anyway," then, on reflection she added, "If this *is* Paradise."

Fin considered what Eden had said, very carefully. It was unlike her to be so negative.

"So maybe it is through the Fountain of Enlightenment that we relieve our doubts and get the answers to all of our questions Eden."

He felt for the key around his neck, as if touching it might unlock the secret of the Fountain. His chin dropped and his eyes widened at the surprise of what he found. It was no longer a key hanging from the chain around his neck, it was a golden goblet!

"Check your key Eden, mine's changed!"

Eden did. It was a golden goblet, just like Fin's, about the size of an egg cup. Eden looked at it in wonderment.

"I think it's time to open Mum's next letter Fin. Perhaps that will help us."

Eden took the letters from her pocket. There were only two left unopened. She selected the one with the number four on it, opened it and took a deep breath and began to read.

"Darling Eden,

If you are reading this letter, then you have safely crossed the arid desert to the Fountain of Enlightenment. But you will not yet have found the gift of enlightenment. To do that, you must drink from the fountain using the magical goblet around your neck.

Together the mystical waters of the fountain and the magic of the goblet, will give you the powers that you need to endure and find the Creator.

You are so very close to me now darling. There are Purple Mountains all around you in the distance. I am somewhere on the other side of those mountains. To get to the Creator, and then to me, you have to cross those mountains. Beyond the mountains, is the Valley of Shadows and beyond that, are the Silver Mountains. Beyond those, is where the Creator is and the key to finding me. The Shadows are evil and deadly, but they cannot cross the Silver Mountains. You will be safe when you are on the other side of them.

I am waiting and praying that you make it through your final challenge. Nobody has ever gone into the Valley of Shadows and come out alive. You must use the powers that you discover at the fountain wisely, so that you don't ever find yourself in the Valley of Shadows. Ever!

It is a long journey on foot darling, but why would you walk there, when you can fly?

Your devoted mother,

Kikki."

"When we can fly?" Fin questioned. "But we can't fly. What did Mum mean by that?"

Eden was ahead of him and already had the answer. Well perhaps she did, she wasn't really that sure.

"I think that once we have drunk water from the fountain, using our golden goblets, we will have the enlightenment that we need. Maybe," she added, with slightly less confidence.

Fin agreed and took both cups to the pool. He dipped them in the crystal clear water and offered one to Eden. The water in the cups began to effervesce and then turned an unappetising fluorescent green.

"I'm not sure about this," Fin said as he raised the glass to his lips, "but it smells delicious. Limes, I think."

They clashed the little goblets together.

"Here goes Fin. Down in one," Eden encouraged, and they did.

The luminescent liquid drained from the goblets, into the parched mouths of the expectant children. They both sneezed involuntarily as the bubbles teased their noses. Moments later, the strange liquid seemed to have charged every cell of their bodies, to the point that it was almost painful.

Bright lights filled their minds, as if a rainbow had exploded in their brains. Their senses had become super heightened. Their ears were filled with the strangest sounds. They could hear things they never could have before, like the beating of their hearts and the sound of a snake slithering across the sand. Their skin had become super sensitive. They could even feel the droplets of their sweat as it ran in little rivers down their bodies. Everything about them was changing.

Eventually the sensations passed but it had left them *different* somehow. They were energised and aware. They looked out into the distance across the purple mountains, which were now crystal clear to their eyes. They could even see the eagles soaring in the air above them, nearly fifty miles away. They were both sensing the possibilities inside their transformed bodies.

"Now I understand why Mum said, *'why would you walk there, when you can fly?'* I really think that we can do anything we want now Eden, anything."

Then Fin did the strangest thing. He bent forwards and hunched his back. Fin looked like he was straining, almost in pain. The back of his t-shirt began to bulge with the pressure of something growing inside it. There was a loud ripping noise as his shirt split right down the back and huge feathered wings unfolded. Fin stood tall again and gave his magnificent wings a single flap. The rush of wind almost blew Eden over. At that very moment, Rags returned and placed himself protectively between the two of them. He yapped menacingly and growled showing his teeth.

"It's alright Rags, it's just Fin," Eden reassured.

"We can do anything that we imagine," Fin said excitedly. "Try it!" Fin insisted, giving Rags a drink from the golden goblet. "You too rags."

Less than a minute later, the three of them were stood together, beating their wings in unison. The desert sand swirled in thick clouds around them. None had ever been so excited. It was way past anything they could ever have imagined.

"Off to the Purple Mountains then?" Fin asked with a twinkle in his eye.

"Off to the mountains Fin, and don't spare your wings!"

Rags just yapped enthusiastically.

"Just think positive thoughts Fin, that's all that we need to do. And you Rags!" Eden added.

Their wings spanned nearly three metres and Rags', two. They beat them slowly at first, feeling their way, then increased the rate. Rags was the first airborne because of his weight and he went flapping off in front, as usual.

"I suppose he will be off chasing birds now," Eden said wryly.

"But he won't catch them, just like he never does," Fin laughed.

They took off together, gaining height rapidly. Soon they were five hundred metres up and heading towards the southernmost peaks of the Purple Mountains.

"After we cross the Valley of Shadows and are safely on the other side of the Silver Mountains, we can fly the perimeter of them safely. Then we just search until we find something that looks like where the Creator might live," Eden shouted over the sound of the rushing air.

"Sounds a good plan," Fin yelled back.

Just then Rags veered off towards a flock of birds that looked like Pink Flamingos, only they were green.

"Don't worry Eden, he will find us," Fin added with some certainty. "He always does."

The fifty miles to the edge of the Purple Mountains only took them two hours. Had they been on foot, it might have taken three days, or more. They were thoroughly worn out though. Beating those enormous wings required a massive amount of effort and they wondered at how little birds could fly for so long. Both thought it too much of a risk to attempt crossing the mountains tired. They decided to be cautious and camp on the desert side overnight, then attempt the crossing in the morning. They couldn't afford the risk of being forced to land in the Valley of Shadows. Nobody had ever survived that, apparently. Besides, Rags hadn't caught them up yet.

They landed rather clumsily, ending up in a heap, on the lower, blue grassy slopes of the mountains.

"That wasn't a landing," Fin laughed, "it was a crash! I'm glad nobody was looking!"

Just then, Rags landed beside them gracefully. He folded his wings professionally and then rolled around the grassy bank, laughing and yapping at the comical sight of his new friends' clumsy landing. Tears of mirth were running down his little black face, drenching his woolly fur. It was quite some time before he was able to control himself. Actually it ended abruptly, as he coughed and sprayed them with green feathers.

"Rags, you didn't actually catch one, did you?" Eden asked in disbelief.

"Of course," he yapped proudly, as if there couldn't be any doubt about it.

Actually, he had only got close enough to get a mouthful of green tail feathers, but he wasn't about to admit that. Instead he revelled in his moment of glory.

The three of them enthused about the wonders and thrills of flying until darkness fell. Rags lived and relived his adventure, each time embellishing it slightly. Eden and Fin graciously allowed Rags his indulgence and Rags rewarded them by conjuring up a meal fit for a king. Of course, all the meat was on the bone and he had the scraps and the bones that were left over.

Chapter 10

Paradise. The Valley of Shadows.

The desert is a cold place at night and the temperature dropped to near freezing. They were all grateful to have big soft, feathery wings to wrap themselves up in against the cold. All three of them slept like the dead until dawn.

Refreshed from their night's sleep, they breakfasted enthusiastically. Again it was by the good grace of their Master Chef, Rags. He had dreamt up a string of the fattest and juiciest pork sausages that you could ever think of. Replete, they began to plan the day.

"We could just about see the tops of the Silver Mountains, before we landed yesterday," Eden began, "I would say that they were twice as far away as the Fountain of Enlightenment is."

"So four hours flight time," Fin calculated. "We were exhausted after only two yesterday. Do you think we will make it without stopping in the Valley of Shadows?"

"We must Fin," Eden replied gravely, "Mum said to not find ourselves there, *ever*."

"What about Rags?" Fin was genuinely concerned for their new little friend.

"I think you will find that Rags would have flown twice as far as us yesterday, chasing those green birds," Eden pointed out. "I think it's us we need to worry about Fin."

It was true and they both knew it. Their plan was to circle up as high as they could over the safety of the Purple Mountains, using the uplift of the thermals just like an eagle does. Then they could fly and glide downhill, conserving energy as they passed safely over the Valley of Shadows. That would give them enough strength for the uphill climb over the Silver Mountains. Simple, they thought.

They set off and rose up the thermoclines much faster than they had imagined they might, reaching a height of three thousand metres. The air was freezing at that altitude, taking away a lot of heat and power from their muscles. Thankfully, it meant that there were no birds for Rags to chase and so they kept together. Rags took the lead, as dogs do, and they began the long glide over the Valley of Shadows. They had to beat their wings much more than they thought they would have to, as they were losing height quickly in the thin air.

Below them, they could see dark shapes scurrying across the valley floor. They were like the shadows of clouds, but there were no clouds in the sky to cast shadows. It went way past creepy.

"What do you think they are?" Fin shouted. "I don't like the look of them."

"Neither do I Fin and they move so fast! Eden had a bad feeling about it.

The sight of what they assumed must be the *Shadows*, filled Eden and Fin with dread. They beat their wings harder to try and gain more height, but the cold and their fear was cramping their muscles. They were tiring fast, much too fast. Rags began to yap urging them on as he sensed the terror rising in them. It seemed like, despite how hard they tried, that the ground was pulling them towards it.

“Look!” Fin pointed at the Shadows directly below them. “They’re grouping together, forming a pack, like wolves.”

“They’re tracking us, waiting for us to land. Oh my God Fin they’re hunting us!”

Then the full horror of it hit them. They were now low enough to see that the Shadows were leaving a trail behind them, like slugs; a trail of death. They were consuming everything in their path. The blue grass and trees had turned brown and putrid, where they had passed over it.

“Fly for your life Eden. Fly for your life!” Fin yelled in desperation.

They tried. They really tried, but it was hopeless. Their wings felt leaden and their lungs were fighting for air. Now they were literally skimming across the menacing Shadows that were only feet below them. The Shadows moved like globules of black oil on a steel tray, so fast and so fluid. The smell of the putrefied grass and trees they had consumed made them gag. The thought that they would soon be part of that same putrid mess, was terrifying. The panic inside them was taking over; it was only a matter of moments now, before it would all be over.

"I'm sorry Mum," Eden said to herself, as if in prayer. "We've failed you."

Her mother's words were clear in her mind, *"You must use the powers that you discover at the fountain wisely, so that you don't ever find yourself in the Valley of Shadows. Ever!"*

While Eden was in that final reverie, she hadn't noticed that one of the Shadows below her had reached up with an oily tendril. It grabbed her ankle viciously. Eden screamed out, as the oil burned through her skin and dissolved half of her shoe. It began to drag her down. She heard Rags growl, like she had never heard him growl before. He swooped down and bit the tendril off, freeing her. Rags yelped in agony, as the oily flesh burned his mouth, terribly.

"Rags!" Eden screamed out, but Rags was lost in the fight to protect her.

She looked back over her shoulder to see him, but he was gone.

"Rags!" Eden screamed again, pitifully. "God help us. Please, somebody help us!"

It was over for them. She knew it and Fin knew it too. Eden was just giving in to the inevitability of it, when she felt strong hands close around her shoulders and a rush of wind from above. A golden woman, with wings thrice the size of hers, was dragging her from certain death. She saw another, a golden man, doing the same for Fin.

“Rags!” she yelled. “You have to get Rags too,” but the winged woman just drove her ever upwards.

That was the last thing that Eden remembered, before the darkness overcame her.

Chapter 11

Paradise. The Silver Mountains.

It was several hours later, when the exhausted youngsters began to awaken from their death-like slumber. The sun was setting behind the Purple Mountains, plunging the Valley of Shadows into an eerie darkness that made the Shadows invisible. They panicked, as they realised their predicament. They were alone without protection from those nightmare monsters.

Eden and Fin drew their knees defensively up to their chests as they sat looking in horror at the blackness below them, waiting for the Shadows to attack. It was some time before they realised that they were sitting on the lower slopes of the Silver Mountain, on the safe side of the valley.

“How did we get here?” Eden asked with a sigh of relief, still confused from the shock and exhaustion of their ordeal.

"The golden angels, I think," Fin wasn't sure if it was a dream.

"Yes! That's it Fin, the angels."

Eden looked around her. The Silver Mountains shone brightly, reflecting the orange glow of the setting sun. The terror of it all came rushing back. Eden screamed out, bursting into tears at the shocking memory of it.

"Rags!" she yelled, desperately.

Fin put his arm around Eden to comfort her.

"Rags is gone Eden. He fought for us, but he's gone."

Fin was trying to be brave, but he felt just the same. They were both desolated at the loss of their faithful and valiant friend.

"No, I'm not," a yapping voice from behind them corrected. "I'm here."

They spun around in astonishment.

"Rags!" Eden exclaimed, "I thought that you... I mean, you were fighting the Shadows and then we..." Eden was lost for words.

"I don't just chase furry critters and birds you know," Rags growled.

It was only for affect though. He was looking forward to some serious hero fussing.

"Oh Rags, I thought we had lost you. You were *so* brave and so amazing. I've never heard of any dog so bold, so courageous, and so selfless; ever."

Eden fussed Rags to death and he LOVED it!

Rags told his story of how he single-doggedly fought the Shadows, distracting them, so that the golden angels could rescue them. He told of the terrible burns to his mouth and paws that the angels had cured somehow, with their magic, and how the angels flew them to the safety of the grassy slopes at the bottom of the Silver Mountains. It was a wonderful story and a lot of it true. Of course, in the telling of it, Rags had embellished the story a little in his favour. No matter, he still was the bravest little black Cockapoo in the world. Any world, come to that; even Paradise!

So, they had made it across the deadly Valley of Shadows but only just. Now, they had to fly over the Silver Mountains to find the Creator, wherever he might be.

They imagined that he might live in a golden palace in the clouds with the most amazing golden gates and the finest statues. It would be guarded, of course, with ten thousand soldiers and dogs. Rags wasn't too happy about this thought. He just growled, showing his teeth. After all, what was a pack of dogs, when he had just defeated the Shadows?

"We will set off at sunrise," Eden decided. "After Rags has made us the most delicious breakfast, of course."

Rags' cuisine had become an expectation.

They talked well into the night. At last exhausted, they cuddled up together, folding their wings around them and fell into a deep sleep. Several hours later, they woke to the smell of cooking bacon. Just the best smell in the world!

"Oh Rags, that smells divine!" Fin enthused. "I hope there's lots of it."

There was, a mountain of it, in freshly baked bread and grilled tomatoes to make it wet and easy to scoff. At last Fin had to admit.

"I think I'm too heavy to fly."

They burnt an extra hour of daylight while they dozed on the slopes, waiting for their breakfast to settle. At last they were up for the adventure. Their plan was to get up high above the mountains, like before, to get a good view of the land that lay beyond; the land of the Creator. They imagined that his enormous palace wouldn't be hard to spot in the clouds, or on the earth, or wherever it might be.

So they set off with brave Rags leading. Their powerful wings, refreshed from their night's sleep, beat rhythmically driving them ever upwards. A flock of pink geese passed below them, in that typical arrow way that they do. Rags desperately fought off the urge to chase them and managed; just. After all, he was the leader of the pack now and with that came great responsibility, Rags conceded.

At last they were as high as they needed to be. The Silver Mountains below them, shone spectacularly in the morning sun.

"Look Fin, they are so beautiful. Have you ever seen anything like it?"

"No, nothing," he confirmed, "just the most beautiful sight."

They shuddered simultaneously as they both thought about the horror that lay in the valley just to the other side of it. They could still see the Shadows slithering across the land, searching for their prey. It sent a chill of dread right through them.

"I hope we don't have to go back that way Eden."

"Me either Fin. Let's not even think about that."

They turned their attention to the land below them on the opposite side of the mountain. The beautiful view seemingly stretched out forever. It was like looking out over the plains of Africa. There were herds of the most colourful animals, grazing on the lush blue grass. There were giraffes, elephants, gazelles and zebras, lions and antelope and rhinos. In fact, every species that you could think of, but in the most glorious colours that you could imagine! The land was rich with trees and bushes, with rivers running through them. And the smells, oh my God the smells!

"The *Garden of Eden*," Fin shouted, above the thumping of their wings, "it's beautiful!"

His smile reflected the joy that was in him.

"It is," Eden agreed, "but no palace," she added disappointedly.

They flew all day following the mountain around. It was the same beautiful scene everywhere they looked, but no palace though. Their disappointment was immense and they were exhausted.

"We will have to land and rest," Eden conceded. "This could take forever."

Rags led them down to the side of a green lake. When they arrived, all the water birds took off in fright. They had never seen such strange beings as the three of them. It was too much for rags though. He was off after them in a flash.

"That's the last we will see of him for a few hours," Fin said with a shrug.

They sat there, considering what to do. They agreed that they could search this wilderness forever and never find the palace.

The land was vast and they were so small. It seemed hopeless. They had come so far on their journey and with such hope, but their spirits were low now.

"We have the last letter to open," Fin pointed out. "Perhaps now is the time?"

"Yes," Eden agreed. "I think you are right Fin."

Eden took the little envelope from her pocket, the one with number five written on it, and kissed it.

"Here goes Fin. This is the one that takes us on the final stage of our journey. It's win or lose now Fin and we can't lose; not after all we have been through," Eden looked solemn as she read the letter.

"Darling Eden,

Well done darling! You are over the Silver Mountains. I can't imagine how you made it and how scared you must have been, crossing that dreadful land of the Shadows.

You are so close now that I can almost smell your beautiful rose fragrance. I imagine too that you feel lost. But look around you Eden. What you see IS creation itself. The apple never falls far from the tree. Open your mind to all possibility. The Creator is all around you. You just have to let him into your heart.

When you do let him into your heart, he will be there to help you. Let him in Eden. Let him in!

Your devoted mother,

Kikki."

Eden turned to Fin in puzzlement.

"What did all that mean Fin?"

"I don't really know," Fin admitted. "But I think Mum was trying to tell us that creation really is all around us and therefor so is the Creator. We just have to let him into our hearts, but how? I don't know."

"Let's explore this beautiful lake. Perhaps the walk around it will inspire us to imagine how we might let the Creator into our hearts," Eden suggested.

They walked for an hour, wondering at the bountiful and beautiful life that surrounded the lake. The abundance of water had attracted them all. Water was the one thing that all the animals needed and it tempted friend and foe to come together, despite the danger. The dark shapes of crocodiles cruised ominously below the surface of the lake, waiting for a careless animal to become their prey. Rags returned panting from yet another fruitless chase and needed a drink.

“Be careful Rags, you don’t know what’s in there,” Eden urged.

Rags took a swift drink, yapped and stood back a respectful distance as a dark and menacing shape cruised by, just below the surface.

The still air was suddenly torn by the roar of some big animal that was clearly in pain. Whatever animal that might have been, caused all the other animals to flee for their lives. Eden and Fin looked around but could see nothing.

“Rags, come here,” Eden ordered.

He obediently came to her side. They were about to take to the air, when another pained roar, shook the very ground they were stood on. It had to be a monster, they agreed and close by. Then, just in front of them, the bushes shook. They found themselves face to face with a man-eating lion. They all froze with fear as they looked at the massive yellow beast in front of them. The lion gave yet another pained roar that shook Rags to his senses.

“Quickly, fly away,” he yapped.

Rags growled back at the lion, showing his fangs, but it was a bit like David and Goliath. There was the world of difference in their sizes.

They were just about to take off, when Eden noticed that the lion was holding one of his front paws off the ground.

"Wait," she cried out, "he's hurt. Can't you see he's in pain?"

"But he will kill us. We can't help him, it's too dangerous," Fin was with Rags on this one.

"And we can't go and leave him like this," Eden was adamant. "I won't go, not while he is in pain."

Eden was trembling like a leaf with the fear of it. Somehow though, she kept managing to put one foot in front of the other, getting closer and closer to the lion. She whispered soothing things like, "I'm not going to hurt you," and "trust me, I want to help you."

"Ridiculous things to say to a beast that was five times bigger than she was," Eden thought.

None the less, she kept walking towards the great yellow lion, which just seemed to get more and more massive as she got closer. His roars seemed to get louder and louder and more menacing too.

At last, they were face to face. Eden held the lion's stare, trying not to show the fear that was consuming her. The lion let out a roar that was so violent; it blew Eden's hair backwards, like she had put her head out of a car window. His breath reeked of his last meal. Eden hoped to God that she wasn't going to be his next.

That fierce roar was followed by a pathetic whimper, as the lion raised his huge yellow paw towards Eden.

“You poor thing,” Eden gasped. “What have you done to yourself?”

Eden could see that his paw was soaked with blood and swollen with infection. There was a thorn, the size of pencil, stuck deep into the soft pad that came out between his claws. It was just like in one of Aesop’s fables that Eden had read at school, the one about *Androcles and the Lion.*

“That story had a happy ending though,” Eden mused. “I hope this one does too.”

Eden offered her cupped hands to the Lion.

“Give me,” Eden commanded, as forcefully as her trembling voice would allow.

The lion placed his painful paw trustingly in Eden’s hands. She could feel it throbbing with the infection. Eden looked into the lion’s vivid blue eyes with a solemn expression.

“You know this is going to hurt a lot, don’t you?” she whispered.

The great beast nodded his shaggy head and blinked twice. It was his way of accepting what was to come. The thorn was slippery with blood and puss from the wound. There was no way that Eden could grip in with her fingers, so she had no choice.

Ignoring the horrible smell of the festering wound, Eden bit heavily on the end of the thorn. Then, in one swift move, she jerked her head upwards and backwards, dragging the thorn out in one. The lion's roar that followed was literally a scream. Eden backed away in terror.

"Eden!" Fin yelled in fear for her safety.

He came running to her defence, despite that fact that it would have been futile. It was unnecessary though, the lion wasn't about to attack his newly found friend.

"Help me Fin, we have to get the poison out of his paw, or he will get very sick."

Eden tore part of the hem off her t-shirt. Then took a green reed from the bank and knotted it around the piece of cotton.

"We need to draw this swab through his wound to clean it," Eden explained.

Eden turned her face to the lion's; whose own was very sad indeed.

"I have to do this. You understand, don't you?" Eden asked.

Again, the lion blinked his eyes twice in acceptance of the inevitable. Eden passed the stiff reed through the lion's wound and then drew the swab through. Just the nastiest stuff that you could imagine came out. It smelled like death. Eden repeated this three more times with fresh reeds and swabs, torn from her t-shirt. Silent tears were running down the lion's yellow face but he didn't flinch or whimper at all.

"You are such a brave boy," Eden cooed.

She could have sworn that he smiled at her.

"There, all done," Eden declared. "Now you must keep licking the wound, it's your natural antiseptic," she said authoritatively.

She had read that somewhere and new it to be true. Then, the most amazing transformation happened in front of their eyes. As they looked at the lion's face, it began to change. The appearance of the lion melted away and was replaced by that of a golden man. He was dressed in a white robe and had the same vivid blue eyes of the lion. Eden and Fin held on to each other in awe and for support. Neither felt scared though, it was like a religious feeling that they were experiencing, not fear.

The African looking surroundings began to become hazy and shimmer, fading away to take on a new form. Moments later, they found themselves in the throne room of a marble palace. Sat there, on the throne in front of them, was the golden man smiling down on them in the most benign way.

"Are you the C-Creator?" Eden stammered.
"I am he," the golden man replied. "Why have you risked all to come to me?" The Creator asked in a deep, gentle but commanding voice.

"It's a long story," Eden began, "And I don't know where to start."

"Why, at the begging," The Creator suggested. "I usually find that is the best place. And you can fold your wings away; you won't need those again."

They did and they just seemed to disappear. Eden and Fin looked around them. They were in the most magnificent room, formed from light blue polished marble. There were colourful statues of the animals they had seen in the wilderness and many more creatures besides that they hadn't. The air was filled with a riot of fragrances, including their own. Music was playing somewhere, everywhere. It seemed like all their senses were being stimulated at once.

"How did we get here?" Fin asked in wonderment.

"Through compassion," the golden man said simply. "You showed compassion for a fellow creature when he needed help. You did it selflessly, despite the danger you were in. That was all you needed to do to find me."

"Fin. Mum said that the Creator was all around us and that we just had to let him into our hearts. Well, that's what we must have done without knowing it."

"Your Mum," The Creator was quick to pick up on it. "Who is your mother?"

"Kikki," Eden offered.

"Not Queen Kikki, surely?" the Creator looked surprised. "I haven't heard of her for years."

"Thirteen, I would guess," Eden said with confidence. "That's how many years I have been gone. And that's when the Murks took her. Right after I was born."

"What do you know of the Murks?" The Creator's mood had changed to one of concern.

"Only that they are evil and a danger to us," Eden answered, "and that they have taken our mother to the Vacuum and many Sensors like her.

"Why might they do that?" the Creator asked.

He clearly didn't know what terrible things had been going on. Fin answered his question.

"They are sealed away in the Vacuum, wherever that is, forever. Eventually, they lose their senses there; sight, smell and taste particularly. But when those have gone and life is empty and bland, they lose their will to live and just die."

"Who told you that?" the golden man looked shocked.

"Muffins," Fin answered, simply.

"So you know Muffins too? I wondered what became of him," The Creator looked pensive. "And why would Muffins come into this?"

Eden interceded. It was going to take forever to explain in questions and answers, she decided.

"I will tell you the story from the beginning, right from when I was a baby until I pulled the thorn out of your foot," Eden declared. And she did.

She told the Creator all about the orphanage in her world, run by the cruel Mrs Jones. She explained how they had trapped her in that Underworld, a place like Purgatory. She told him about Muffins, his briefcase and the envelopes from their mother.

She told him how their father, and other fathers from Paradise, had gone to rescue their children from the orphanages that the Murks had taken over. She told him how the Murks had tricked them into going through the wrong gateway, sending them to the Underworld, instead of the orphanage.

"They had painted the gateways in opposite colours, you see. The gold one black and the black one, gold," Fin explained. "The colour that should have taken them to us, took them to that hellish place instead; forever."

"Not necessarily *forever* Fin," the Creator corrected, offering them a glimmer of hope. "What if they never went there in the first place? What if you could stop them going through the wrong gateway?"

"But they've already gone. How could we?" Fin lamented.

"Could it be by opening our minds and imagination to all possibilities, like our mother suggested?" Eden asked, but she already knew that it was so.

"It's exactly that," the Creator clapped his hands in glee. "Imagine yourself back in time to just before your father and the other men enter the gateway. Perhaps you could stop them somehow."

"We could warn them and say that..." Fin began, but the Creator stopped him.

"No Fin, there are rules with time. You can go back, but you would just be a visitor there. Your time is here and now. They wouldn't be able to see you, but you could affect things. You just have to use your imagination."

The Creator was all knowledgeable on this, as he had set those rules. He continued.

"The other thing that you must know, is that if you succeed in changing the future, you will not be able to come back to your own time. Everything will have changed, you would have changed. You would become of that time Eden, you a baby and Fin, a one-year old. All that has happened to you will just be memories of what might have been. Could you live with that?" He asked, cocking an inquisitive eyebrow.

Eden and Fin looked at each other for a long moment, before nodding.

"Yes," they said emphatically.

The Creator smiled his benign smile. It was just as he had hoped. He looked sad though and Eden picked up on it.

"Why do you look so sad?" Eden asked.

"Because I created all this, so I am responsible," the Creator gestured with his arms all around him. "I created the Sensors and the Murks too, in a world where all things were equal. I gave them all freedom of choice, which is the biggest gift of all. It seems that the Murks must have misused that gift and tipped the balance of power their way."

The Creator sighed and sat down. He looked like the burden of this new knowledge had aged him.

"Alas, I cannot intercede," he lamented. "The rules forbid such things, even though those rules are of my making."

His words and sadness brought out Eden's positivity.

"Fin and me will go back and fix this, somehow," Eden assured him, although she hadn't a clue how. "We will bring the Murks back under control and restore that balance."

They were brave words for a little girl, but her heart was big enough to make it happen.

"After all, I am a princess," Eden thought, "and with that comes great responsibility too!"

They spent the rest of the day and night with the Creator. In that time, he taught them so much about life, both in Paradise and in general. They had become the best of friends. It was after breakfast the next day when Eden decided that it was time to go. She had spent many hours thinking about what they were going to do to save their father and the other men. Eden took the Creator's hand.

"It really has been the loveliest time here with you in this palace, but we have to go while we still have enough courage to do so," Eden began. "Can you take us back to the wilderness now, so that we can continue our journey please?"

The Creator nodded his shaggy head sadly, he would miss them. As he did so, it began to transform. Slowly, the gold turned to yellow and his features elongated. Moments later, they were looking into the vivid blue eyes of the great yellow lion. He greeted them with his most menacing roar. This time, none of them even flinched. The lion laughed in the human way.

"I guess I'm no longer frightening to you," the Creator conceded.

"No," Fin agreed. "Not now that we know you are just a great big soft pussycat. But I was the first time I saw you though; very!" he admitted.

The Creator roared another laugh, and then began his goodbyes. Eden could have sworn that a little tear of regret escaped from one of his friendly blue eyes.

"I will leave you both," the Creator began.

Rags yapped in annoyance at the Creator's oversight.

"Oh and of course you too Rags," he added with a laugh.

The Creator gave Rags a big friendly lick on his face. Rags sneezed at the tickle of it and jumped up to try and do the same. The lion was tall though and Rags missed, falling in an untidy heap at the lion's feet. They all laughed, even Rags.

"I will bid the *three* of you goodbye then. It saddens me that you are leaving, but I feel richer for knowing you and wish you all the luck that you will need to fulfil your quest. The Murks would be wise not to underestimate the Prince and Princess of Paradise. Nor you Rags," he added with a chuckle.

With that, the great yellow lion faded into the background of the wilderness, but his memory would be in their hearts forever.

Chapter 12

Paradise. The gateway, the *true* 'Key of Destiny'.

And so Eden, Fin and Rags found themselves alone in the wilderness once more. They were a little bit scared, a little bit unsure of themselves, but very excited! This was to be the final step in their quest to free their mother and father from the claws of the Murks. It was their chance to finally fulfil their destiny. It was their chance to take the power away from the Murks, freeing the Kingdom of Paradise from their cruel tyranny. If they succeeded, families would be re-united and happiness would be brought back to the land. They could not fail. They must not fail. It all rested on their shoulders now and theirs alone.

Eden and Fin both found the moment immense. Rags sensed it too.

"Where is it that you want me to take you?" Rags yapped.

He had anticipated that they were going on another journey.

"Yes, where are we going?" Fin was also in the dark.

"Well," Eden replied, "back to the only place where we can make a difference; back to the gateway where we came into this world."

"How do we make a difference?" Fin asked.

"It's the same place that our father and the other men went to when they tried to rescue us from the Murks," Eden began. "That time, they went the wrong way. Now we are going to fix it so that they don't."

"And do you know how we get there and go back in time?" Fin challenged. "I for sure, don't."

It was one of the things that Eden had considered very carefully and all crystal clear in her mind. She turned to Rags.

"Rags, you don't need to actually take us to the gateway, you just have to help us imagine that we are all there together," Eden explained. "I want us to all imagine that we are there *thirteen* years ago, at the same time that the Murks painted the trapdoors."

"What then?" Fin asked. "The Creator said that Dad and the others wouldn't be able to see us because we wouldn't be in their time. How can we warn them?"

It was good logic, but Eden had the answer.

"We don't have to Fin; we just have to paint the gateways back to their true colours when the Murks leave. That way, Dad and the others will go through the right gateway and not to that terrible place. None of this will ever have happened, don't you see?"

"Brilliant!" Fin exclaimed, clapping his hands together. "Let's do it.

"OK," Eden said, picking up Rags. "Hold my hand Fin. I want to make sure that we all stay together on this journey and end up in the same place. Mum and the Creator both told us to use our imaginations and possibility, so here goes everything!"

They linked their minds and imagined the place where they had entered this world of Paradise. They imagined the blue grass, red trees and the two trapdoors in the grass; one of them gold, and the other black. They imagined the two rusty tins of gold and black paint with their hard, paint-dried paintbrushes on top of them, next to the red tree. Now this was the clever bit. They then imagined that the tins were not rusty and that the paintbrushes were still wet with fresh paint. The wilderness around them began to fade. It felt like they were being spun around backwards, like the hands of a clock in super-fast reverse.

Right when they thought they couldn't stand the spinning motion any longer, it stopped. It took a few minutes more for their heads to follow suit though.

When, eventually, they could open their eyes without feeling sick, they found themselves stood between the gold and black trapdoors that were the gateways into two entirely different words. The paint on them was still fresh and wet. They looked around and there, beside the red tree, were the two shiny tins of paint with their wet paintbrushes perched on top. In the distance, was a group of a dozen or so men running away at a pace.

"Murks," Fin spat out the word disdainfully. "They have laid their trap, and now the cowards are running away to watch from a distance."

At that moment, Rags spotted a little purple furry thing and was off on the chase. To Rags' surprise, the little critter didn't run. Rags skidded to a stop next to it and barked menacingly. Still the furry little animal didn't run, nor pay any attention to him at all.

"It can't see you Rags," Eden observed, "It's just like the Creator said. We are invisible in this time."

Rags turned around disappointedly and returned to his friends.

"I would have caught him," he growled, more to himself than to anyone else.

"So, if the little animal can't see Rags, neither will the Murks, nor our people see us," Eden deduced. "That means we are safe to execute our plan."

With that, Eden picked up the paint and brushes. She gave Fin the black paint and brush.

"Fin. You paint the gold trapdoor back to black, while I paint the black one, gold."

They worked quickly. Ten minutes later, the gateways were once again in their correct colours. Fin smiled as he felt the chain around his neck. The golden challis was once again a key.

"I'm going to open the trapdoor that leads to the orphanage, so that when Dad and the others arrive, they can get to safety quickly. I don't trust those Murks. They might come back."

"Good idea Fin, we can't be too careful."

Fin entered his key in the lock of the golden trapdoor and opened it. Just then, an army of men on horseback appeared on the horizon. The air became filled with the sound of their hooves as they thundered towards them. Leading them was a dark haired, handsome man with a strong chin. He wore a golden crown and carried his sword high, as he charged on to the gateway.

Eden and Fin looked on in awe. They had never seen so many men. Their father must have called on every able bodied man in Paradise to fight against the Murks and free their children.

The King dismounted in a single fluid move, landing lightly on the floor. It was something that you would think unlikely for such a big and strong man.

"Follow me," he commanded.

The King threw open the golden trapdoor that led to the orphanage. It was amazing to watch. Their father disappeared down the gateway in seconds, followed by his men. It was like watching water flowing down the plug hole. The army of men just slipped away into that other world until they were all gone. The only evidence that it had happened, was the sight of a thousand horses grazing peacefully on the lush blue grass.

“Fin, wasn’t Dad handsome and so manly?” Eden yearned to run after him but it would have been pointless.

“Yes,” Fin agreed. “He looked a lot like me didn’t you think?” Fin quipped and grinned broadly.

Neither could truly begin to imagine how terrible it would have been if they had watched their father, and that many men, pour into that dreadful Underworld. They pulled away from that thought and allowed themselves the luxury of a laugh. Their laugh was short lived though. Appearing on the hill, were thousands of Murks in hot pursuit of their prey. Fin ran to the golden trapdoor and locked it, then opened the lock on the black one.

“This will hasten the Murks’ entry into the Underworld!” he yelled.

Eden called out to him to hurry back, although she wasn’t sure what difference that might make. Rags yapped his encouragement for good measure.

The Murks swarmed by and disappeared down the black trapdoor, just as rapidly as their father’s men had down the golden one. In the excitement of the pursuit, the Murks were making so much noise that they couldn't hear the dreadful screams of the men who had gone through the trapdoor before them. An hour later, there wasn't a Murk in sight.

Eden and a Fin ran over and slammed the heavy door shut behind them, sealing the Murks in. Fin locked it with his golden key and it was done. Rags jumped excitedly up into Eden's arms and joined in for the celebration that never happened.

There was a consequence to changing history, just as the Creator had warned them. Eden, Fin and Rags found themselves in a time where they no longer belonged, where they couldn't stay. From the moment that their father and his men entered the trapdoor to safety, the sequence of events that followed would never be the same. They had changed history and there was no place there for them now.

All of a sudden, they felt like they were falling into the blackness of a deep, bottomless pit. Eden, not understanding what was happening, immediately feared that the trapdoor to the Underworld had collapsed beneath them.

"Fin! Rags!" Eden screamed. But it was in vain, as neither replied.

Chapter 13

Paradise. The home-coming.

"Muffins," the enchanting voice of a young woman called out.

A bespectacled little man with a magnificent handlebar moustache appeared. He wore a bowler hat and a waistcoat with pocket watch and chain.

"You called your highness," Muffins answered, as he bowed respectfully.

"Ah, there you are dear Muffins."

The beautiful woman smiled at him affectionately. Her golden blonde hair was a mass of curls and her eyes, of emerald green, shone with happiness. And why shouldn't they? She had just brought a beautiful daughter into the world.

"Would you call the King and have him bring the Prince to meet his sister?" she asked.

Queen Kikki had just the most radiant smile on her face. Muffins always found it an immense pleasure to serve her. In fact it was what he lived for and all that he knew.

Muffins walked briskly out of the room brimming with the pleasure of being the one chosen to announce the Princess's arrival. The plump little man scuttled down the corridors to the Kings royal chambers, knocked and opened the door to the King's command.

“Muffins, do you bring me good news?” the King asked, a little nervously.

“I do indeed, your highness. Queen Kikki and the baby Princess are awaiting you and the young Prince,” Muffins couldn’t have looked more proud.

“Splendid news!” the King exulted and immediately looked more at ease.

He picked the infant Prince up in his strong arms and hoisted him above his head.

“Did you hear that Fin? You have a baby sister!”

The King settled Fin into his arm and strode off briskly down the corridors to meet his daughter for the first time. Poor old Muffins could barely keep up with him, despite his little legs scurrying away frantically beneath him.

“Most undignified,” he muttered.

The King threw the doors open into the Queen’s chamber. Before him, was his wife looking radiant, holding a pink bundle in her arms and the room was filled with the sweet scent of roses.

“Darling!” the King called out in the genuine pleasure of seeing her. “You look amazing. Let me see her.”

The King dropped to his knee next to his Queen. He kissed her, and then opened the pink bundle, so that he could see his daughter's face for the first time.

"Oh, she's beautiful, just like you Kikki," he meant every word of it.

"Why thank you kind sir," Queen Kikki replied, blushing a little.

"Have you given her a name yet? "the King asked, raising a curios dark brow.

"Yes, Eden," she smiled at Fin who was curiously reaching out to his new-born sister. "Meet your sister Fin. This is Eden. I hope you have many adventures together."

Queen Kikki had no way of knowing that they already had!

At that moment a little black dog scampered in excitedly. He came straight up to Eden to smell her.

"And this is Rags, Eden. He will be your faithful friend for many years to come," Queen Kikki promised.

Rags yapped his approval and bundled in to be part of that happy family circle, one that even the Murks could not destroy. It was all thanks to Eden Rose Lock.

The End

AUTHOR's NOTE

I hope that you enjoyed reading 'Eden and the Key of Destiny' as much as I enjoyed writing it for you.

If you did, I would be forever grateful if you could leave a review on Amazon for me, so that others might be encouraged to read it too. Tell your friends as well please!

Thank you.

Chris Savage

Printed in Poland
by Amazon Fulfillment
Poland Sp. z o.o., Wrocław

51050699R00070